Y0-BTW-399

He reminded her of a soap star she'd once drooled over

Zane's dark hair was tousled, as if from sleep, while his eyes had that squinty bedroom look that came from the day's first exposure to bright light. And he wasn't wearing a shirt.

God help her, he looked glorious without one.

Naomi saw the delicious dip where his biceps met his shoulder, and the smooth bulges of his pecs. Beautiful was one of the many words she could think of to describe him.

Hot, delicious and tempting were a few others.

"You wanted to talk," he said, "so go ahead and talk."

"I was hoping we could sit and have a civilized conversation."

He looked at her long and hard, then gave a slow smile that probably was meant to warn her. Warn her that if she came in, he couldn't be responsible for what happened next.

Who said this man needed to be made over? He had her captivated, and he wasn't even fully dressed.

Dear Reader,

I've always loved makeovers. Even as a kid, I drew "before" and "after" pictures—stick people with bad hair and makeup, transformed by my third-grade artistic skills into more stylish, well-coiffed versions of themselves.

So when the idea came to me for the story *Sexy All Over*, I couldn't wait to have fun with my heroine, who does makeovers for a living. I quickly found, though, that the story had a mind of its own, and that our commonly held ideas of perfection aren't necessarily what we should strive for. Consider the hero, Zane Underwood, for instance. He is far from perfect, but he's oh-so-appealing in his imperfection. I'd take him over Mr. Perfect in an "after" photo any day, and so, my heroine learns, would she.

I'd love to hear what you think of *Sexy All Over*, so drop me a note at jamie@jamiesobrato.com or visit my Web site, www.jamiesobrato.com, to learn more about me and my upcoming books.

Sincerely,

Jamie Sobrato

Books by Jamie Sobrato

HARLEQUIN BLAZE

HARLEQUIN TEMPTATION

JAMIE SOBRATO

Sexy All Over

TORONTO • NEW YORK • LONDON
AMSTERDAM • PARIS • SYDNEY • HAMBURG
STOCKHOLM • ATHENS • TOKYO • MILAN • MADRID
PRAGUE • WARSAW • BUDAPEST • AUCKLAND

If you purchased this book without a cover you should be aware that this book is stolen property. It was reported as "unsold and destroyed" to the publisher, and neither the author nor the publisher has received any payment for this "stripped book."

To the Temptresses,
one of the smartest, funniest, most talented group of women
I've ever had the pleasure of knowing

ISBN 0-373-79194-1

SEXY ALL OVER

Copyright © 2005 by Jamie Sobrato.

All rights reserved. Except for use in any review, the reproduction or utilization of this work in whole or in part in any form by any electronic, mechanical or other means, now known or hereafter invented, including xerography, photocopying and recording, or in any information storage or retrieval system, is forbidden without the written permission of the publisher, Harlequin Enterprises Limited, 225 Duncan Mill Road, Don Mills, Ontario, Canada M3B 3K9.

All characters in this book have no existence outside the imagination of the author and have no relation whatsoever to anyone bearing the same name or names. They are not even distantly inspired by any individual known or unknown to the author, and all incidents are pure invention.

This edition published by arrangement with Harlequin Books S.A.

® and TM are trademarks of the publisher. Trademarks indicated with ® are registered in the United States Patent and Trademark Office, the Canadian Trade Marks Office and in other countries.

www.eHarlequin.com

Printed in U.S.A.

1

WHEN NAOMI TYLER found her boyfriend sitting naked at her computer in the middle of the night, she first thought he'd gotten lost on the way to the bathroom.

But it only took a few squinty-eyed seconds for the *naked* truth to reveal itself.

Moments ago, she'd awoken to the inexplicable sound of heavy breathing coming from the living room, which was only one room away in her small apartment.

The glowing red numbers on the alarm clock had told her it was three in the morning, exactly two and a half hours before she had to be awake to prepare for a meeting with her most important client.

Soft light poured through the open bedroom door.

A moan reached her. And then, "Oh yeah, ohhhh…"

Jackson's voice. A glance at the space next to her had confirmed that he wasn't in bed, and the disoriented fog had begun to lift from her brain.

She'd sat up, her heart pounding. Why was her boyfriend up at this time of night, and why was he moaning? She'd slipped out of bed and gone to the door, afraid of what she might find. If he had another woman in her apartment…

Not possible. Jackson was sweet, loyal, faithful.

And sitting at her computer naked.

Now, she blinked at the sight of him on the other side of the living room, lit by the glow of her computer monitor. His blond hair had taken on a weird greenish tinge from the screen, and his hand was moving in his lap, his noises growing more urgent by the second.

His free hand was on the keyboard. With both hands he quickly typed something, then returned to his task.

What the hell?

A wave of nausea rose in her stomach, but she froze, unable to make a sound or move. A silly bit of advice from *Cosmo* played in her head—*if you find him masturbating, join in and help him out. He'll think it's a huge turn-on.*

Okay, fine. Maybe a turn-on for him, but Naomi was too pissed about having her sleep interrupted by his little rendezvous with the computer to work up any sort of amorous feelings.

She was considering slipping back into the bedroom and trying to get some sleep when his moaning reached its inevitable crescendo, and his grand finale ended with something oozing down the monitor.

An urge to retrieve the Windex from the kitchen nearly overtook her, as her emotions spiraled from shocked to disgusted to embarrassed in the space of a few seconds. But she suppressed her neatnik urge and decided the best way to face this little problem was head-on.

She coughed, and Jackson nearly jumped out of her desk chair, which she made a mental note to give a good scrubbing tomorrow.

"Naomi!"

"What are you doing?" she blurted. "No, don't answer that. I see what you're doing."

Jackson heaved a sigh and looked at his hand, then at the computer monitor.

"Tissues are on the left."

"I was just, um, instant messaging with a friend."

"Instant messaging? Naked? At 3:00 a.m.?"

"It's nothing, just a little cybersex," he said, taking a different tack now—the casual, guilt-free male.

Naomi watched as he wiped off the monitor. She tried not to feel disgusted, wishing she could be a sexually enlightened *Cosmo* girl. But mostly she was just pissed off.

"We haven't had sex in weeks. Why aren't you having sex with me instead of some girl—it is a girl, right?—on the computer?"

"Of course it's a girl."

"How can you be sure?"

He looked confused. "She e-mailed me a picture."

Her temper flared. "You're probably getting it on with some middle-aged, hairy guy."

He gaped at her as if he'd never considered the possibility.

"Why not with me?" she asked, her voice revealing too much emotion. "Do I bore you?"

Silence.

"Do I?"

A guilty look crossed his face, and he shrugged.

Shrugged?

Shrugged.

Naomi was so very wide awake now. "Get the hell out of my apartment!" she screeched.

"Naomi, you're not boring. I'm just tired, okay? Can we talk about this tomorrow after we've both had some rest?"

"Tired? You weren't too tired to jerk off on my computer, but you're too tired to talk? Get out!" She pointed a finger at the door. "Now!"

He stood and came toward her, all of a sudden looking far more ridiculous than sexy in his naked state. "Can I at least get my clothes?"

She marched into the bedroom, fueled by fury and wounded pride. Jackson's clothes, predictably, lay in a pile on the floor. She scooped them up, along with his shoes, went to the second-story window, opened it, and dropped everything onto the lawn below.

She turned to Jackson. "Your clothes are waiting for you downstairs. Now get out!"

"SO THEN THE BASTARD LEFT, and I was wide awake for the rest of the night."

Naomi took a long drink of her iced tea, wishing she'd ordered something a little more caffeinated. She'd been dragging all morning and still had another client to meet after lunch. Her best friend Talia Ramsey sat across the table from her at their favorite lunch spot, trying hard not to laugh.

"I'm sorry, sweetie. I'm just so proud of you for making him leave naked."

Naomi was absolutely sure she wasn't boring in bed.

Well, mostly sure…

Okay, not sure at all. She liked sex as much as the next girl, but maybe she'd been working too hard lately, focusing a little too much on her career. And maybe she'd let her sex life slide.

"What if he's right?" Naomi said.

"Frankly, I'm a little surprised Jackson even knows where his penis is, let alone has any ideas about what to do with it."

Naomi leaned in and whispered, "We've had *sex!* Of course he knows what to do with it."

Talia looked unconvinced. She'd never been crazy about Jackson, and now Naomi knew that in the future she should just trust her friend's gut reactions to men the same way she could trust her own gut reactions about how people should present themselves to the world.

Too bad her instincts could never see past the surface of people to the cybersex-obsessed weirdos that lurked within.

"I know you think you were having sex, but really, you've slept with what, five guys? How can you be sure?"

"You're keeping count?"

Talia shrugged. "Old habit. The important thing is, could he give you an orgasm every time?"

The guy at the next table looked over at them and smiled. Even if their conversation hadn't centered around sex, men never could help staring at Talia. She had pale blond hair that fell past the middle of her back, silvery blue eyes and a sense of fashion that accentuated her strong, statuesque figure. Today she wore a head-turning fitted white business suit with a skirt that was about a half inch away from being improper for work.

"Could you lower your voice?"

"Could he?" Talia demanded, oblivious to Naomi's protests.

"Every time is a tad unrealistic, don't you think?"

"Not at all."

"He did once," she admitted. "Almost."

Talia gave her a knowing look. "Almost doesn't count with orgasms."

"Don't they get extra points for effort?"

She shook her head.

"If he's nice, respectful, intelligent and good looking, I can take care of myself," Naomi said, then lowered her voice. "With regard to *other* matters."

"Have you ever had an orgasm with a guy?" Talia asked, finally whispering low enough so no one else could hear.

Naomi felt her cheeks warming. She had no reason to be embarrassed, did she? It wasn't her fault all her boyfriends seemed confounded by the clitoris, mystified by the G-spot. "I've had…" A few, she almost said, which would have been a lie. And she made it a rule not to lie to her friends. "Okay, none."

The expression on Talia's face would have been more appropriate for the news that a loved one had died. "Oh, sweetie! You don't know what you're missing out on."

"An orgasm's an orgasm," Naomi whispered. "What difference does it make if I have them with a guy or with me, myself and I?"

Her friend's eyebrows shot up. "Are you serious?"

"Of course I am. I don't see how it matters."

"It's like the difference between taking a warm bath and getting into a bubbling hot tub. They're both nice, but one's a lot more exhilarating than the other."

Had Naomi really been missing out on the bubbling hot tub of sexual experiences for all this time?

She frowned and tried to ignore the nagging feeling that Talia was right.

Naomi had been missing out.

She was nearly thirty, and all this time, she'd never taken a dip in a hot tub. She glanced down at the club sandwich she hadn't touched yet and felt like throwing it across the room.

"Are you sure it's that much better for everyone? Maybe it's just you, or the guys you've been sleeping with."

"Naomi." Talia gave her the look. The look that said she'd lost her mind. "If it was just as good alone as it is with a partner, then we wouldn't need men until we were ready to pop out babies. Why do you think people even have recreational sex?"

Naomi gave the question some serious thought. "For the intimate contact?"

"For the industrial-grade orgasms."

"I can't be this naive." Could she? "I mean, how could I be the only person on earth who doesn't know about this?"

"Because you were raised by Senator Atchison Tyler, the man who wrote the book on being virtuous?"

Literally. Her father had written a bestselling book on how to lead a morally conscious life, entitled *The Angel On Your Shoulder.*

She made a face. "I actually believed when I was a kid that there was an angel camped out on my shoulder at all times. But she wasn't there to give me advice or watch out for my well-being—she was acting as my spiritual tattletale."

"I'm sure the nunnery where you got your education didn't help."

Talia took a sip of her white wine, somehow managing not to get even a speck of her pink lipstick on the glass.

"It wasn't a nunnery—it was an all-girls academy."

"Same difference. The point is, you're warped, and as your best friend I've always felt it's my personal duty to unwarp you."

"You have?"

"I thought I'd done a pretty good job until now."

"Give me a little credit. I can walk into Victoria's Secret and actually buy lingerie now without feeling weird."

"Okay, okay, and you made good progress at Ally's bachelorette party last fall."

Naomi winced at the memory of drinking way too much and dancing like a complete idiot with a male stripper. She'd starred in her own personal 1980s party movie.

"Progress is not tucking dollar bills in a strange man's G-string."

"You have your definition, and I have mine." Talia smiled, and then her smile transformed into a wicked grin. "I've got the best idea ever."

"About?"

"Your orgasm problem. I know just the guy for you."

"Oh no, you don't. I'm not enduring another one of your matchmaking attempts."

"I've only ever set you up with a guy once, and that was just so I could get an in with his friend. Now this will be an entirely different kind of setup."

"Different how?"

"Ken is the kind of guy women call for one reason and one reason only."

"Dare I ask?"

"He's the king of all booty calls."

"I am *so* not going to make a booty call."

"Naomi. Just listen. This guy can give you an orgasm just by breathing on you. Seriously, he's the master."

Naomi shifted in her seat and finished off the last of her iced tea. It wasn't sweet the way she loved it, but she'd learned to endure drinking it without sugar for the sake of her no-longer-twenty-year-old thighs.

"Forget about it!"

"Do you want to risk walking around for the rest of your life never having an orgasm with a guy?"

Did she?

"You're being ridiculous. Sooner or later I'll find a guy who understands female equipment."

Or would she? Maybe her equipment was the problem. Maybe *she* was the reason she'd never been able to come with a guy.

Talia saw the doubt in her eyes. "What?"

"What if it's me? What if I'm frigid?"

"Don't be silly. But with Booty Call Ken, you'll know for sure. I can't imagine he's ever left a woman unsatisfied."

Naomi truly had reached a point of desperation when one of Talia's wild ideas wasn't sounding all that ridiculous.

"What does he look like?"

"Remember Luke Duke from *The Dukes of Hazzard?*"

"He does not look like Luke Duke!"

Talia nodded her head, smiling. "Oh yes, my dear. He does."

Naomi sighed. Luke Duke had been the fantasy man of her childhood, before her parents decided that watching *The Dukes of Hazzard* was a morally bankrupt activity. "I'll think about it, but no planning anything without my approval."

"I'll give you twenty-four hours to decide. If you don't get back to me by then, I'm calling Ken and giving him your address."

"You are not. You'll wait until you hear from me, or you'll never see your favorite Kate Spade bag again in this lifetime."

"Fine, if you want to play dirty. I'm just looking out for your best interests." Talia stabbed a leaf of lettuce with her fork. "Now, what are you going to do about Jackson?"

"We're through." Naomi could hardly believe she managed to sound so sure of herself. She'd been dating Jackson for nearly a year, had entertained more than a few notions of him being The One, and now, within the space of twelve hours, she'd decided she never wanted to see him again?

It was an awfully drastic move for her.

"You're dumping him," Talia said, barely containing her laughter. "Over a little sperm on your computer?"

"You're not funny."

"I may not like him, but I know how you felt about him until this morning. Are you sure you won't regret this later?"

"Why are you defending him all of a sudden?"

"I'm not. I just know how you can second-guess yourself. I'm trying to circumvent the midnight phone calls to my apartment."

"He basically told me I'm boring in bed. What's to second-guess?"

"He didn't say that though, did he? He was busted, and guys never know the right thing to say when they're busted."

"He shrugged!"

"I know, it was an asshole thing to do. But he's a guy. By definition, he touches himself, and he's constantly looking for visual stimulus to make touching himself more enjoyable. You shouldn't take it personally."

"I have no problem with the touching part. It's the part about him having cybersex with some other woman that bugs me."

Talia shrugged. She had a way of being horribly jaded when it came to men. "At least it wasn't someone he knew, right?"

"As far as I can tell—no. But who knows how many times they'd done it before I caught him?"

Talia took a bite of her salad. She'd long ago given up believing there were any good men left, and now Naomi felt like a complete idiot for having tried to convince her over the past year that Jackson was one of the last available good ones.

"I'm totally supportive of your dumping him. I just want you to be sure of your reasons."

"It's like he cheated. Sort of—I mean, at what point does this kind of thing become cheating?"

Talia frowned. "When he starts humping your monitor?"

"I'm serious. *Is* it cheating if a guy has cybersex?"

"I don't know. How do you keep typing if you're, um—"

"I saw Jackson take a quick break from the action to type two-handed."

"You're kidding."

"Nope."

Talia narrowed her eyes and stared off out the window at the passing midday traffic. "What makes a person sexy in the cyber world? The ability to type fast?"

"If so, my great-aunt Nell the secretary would be very popular. She can type eighty words per minute."

Talia made a tiger sound in the back of her throat, and the guy at the next table eyed her with renewed interest. Naomi tried to resist descending into a fit of giggles but failed. This was why she loved Talia—she could make her feel as though she were a goofy teenager without all the fears and insecurities.

Until today. Today, Naomi was the new headquarters for Insecurities Incorporated, all because some guy preferred a faceless stranger on the Internet for sex over her.

She was going to change that, even if it meant sleeping with Booty Call Ken. But preferably not. There had to be a better way to prove she was good in bed, and Naomi was going to find it.

She glanced at her watch and saw that if she didn't leave now, she'd be late for her next appointment. "Thanks for meeting me so last-minute. I've gotta run."

"One more thing—if you're really dumping Jackson, make a clean break."

"Got it."

"Seriously. No regrets, Naomi. I don't want to hear a single doubt next time we talk. I just want to hear that you're ready for your first booty call."

Naomi waved and headed for the door. No doubts, no regrets. She could do that, right? Of course.

But already, there was a niggling doubt. What if,

once she'd proven she was good in bed, she started wanting Jackson back? What if the desire to prove herself to *him* became overwhelming?

She left the café and weaved her way through the afternoon lunch crowd on the sidewalk. As she walked, the doubts grew and grew.

Then a plan came to her, fully formed and laid out, ready for her to execute. She'd find a talented guy—whether it be Booty Call Ken or someone of her own choosing—and she'd hone her sexual skills until she was the kind of lover guys never strayed from.

Then she'd show Jackson exactly what he was going to miss out on for the rest of his long, pitiful life.

2

ZANE UNDERWOOD WATCHED the TV monitor as a series of gunshot blasts turned the scene on the darkened streets of Aden into chaos. People ran for cover, and his own voice had taken on a desperate, breathless quality as he reported the progress of the event. He could remember all too well the shock of what happened a moment later, when his cameraman was hit in the shoulder by a stray bullet.

As soon as the memory came to him, the event was reflected on-screen. The sound of machine-gun fire, a cry of pain, and the camera that had been focused on the unrest instantly hit the ground.

The monitor screen went blue.

"You're damn lucky Carlson survived. You shouldn't have been in there," Jack Hiller said, his bald head glistening in the halogen lights of his office. He propped his elbows on the glossy cherry conference table that separated them and leaned in closer. "You know Yemen's swarming with terrorists."

Which was exactly why they should be there,

Zane resisted pointing out. The news manager had made up his mind, and when Jack had an opinion about something, he rarely wavered from it.

"I regret putting Elliot Carlson in danger. But he's a big boy. He knew what he was getting into when he volunteered to cover the story with me."

"I'll be straight with you, Underwood. Your job is in danger. Mediacom doesn't want cowboy journalists."

Zane cringed at the label. "I wasn't the one slinging guns there, Jack."

"You know what I mean. You're too cocky. You're pissing people off."

"We were the first network to cover the story, and it had a direct impact on U.S. naval ships in that area. This isn't really about Yemen, is it?"

"Of course not, but you haven't let me finish."

Zane leaned back in his seat. Here it came….

"You've created an international scandal with that princess. Can't you keep your tool in the tool belt for one damn week?"

He stared at Jack, doing his best to look contrite.

"Have you seen photos of her? She's a knockout," he said, doubtful it was going to count for much.

The "she" in question was Zahara Karim, one of the many daughters of the king of a small Middle Eastern country, which made her a princess. And what a naughty princess she was. She'd been traveling with her father in Yemen for a political visit when she and Zane had bumped into each other in the hotel lobby, and the rest was tabloid headlines.

His first royalty, and probably his last, too, considering the uproar that had erupted when the princess's father found out about their indiscretion.

Zane had barely made it out of Yemen before someone had a chance to lock him up and throw away the key.

No amount of arguing that the king's archaic attitudes about women and virginity were straight out of the Middle Ages could have gotten him out of that mess.

"I don't care if she's the hottest woman in Yemen, you can't go around—"

"Calm down. I think I've learned my lesson."

Not that he considered no more getting naked with princesses in the royal limousine to be that relevant a lesson to learn in the overall scheme of his life, but hey—a guy never knew when such a lesson would come in handy.

"Have you? I heard you say that last year, too, and yet here we are again, having the same conversation."

"This is all about politics, and you know it."

"No, it's about the bottom line."

Zane expelled a pent-up breath. That was one of the biggest lies he'd heard all week. Everything at Mediacom was about the bottom line, and everything was *also* about politics.

"You have my sincere and heartfelt apology, okay?"

"This whole renegade-reporter kick of yours has to stop."

Zane debated whether or not to point out that viewers liked his style. That wasn't why he reported the way he did, but he wasn't altogether ignorant of the fact that he added a little excitement to the news.

What the hell. "I don't think I'm hurting your ratings."

Jack's neck turned red. "You've been in this business—what, ten years?" Zane nodded, and Jack continued. "I've been in it for thirty, and one thing that's been proven time and again is that what viewers want in a news channel is consistency, reliability and balanced news."

"Then how do you explain my popularity?"

"You're not popular, you're controversial. Controversy breeds temporary interest, not long-term viewer loyalty."

"If the truth is controversial, then we should be happy for the controversy."

"The truth is as subjective as anything else. You know that."

Zane had abandoned any boyish ideas of truth coming before all else in journalism years ago. But it was still the value he held most dear. He just avoided talking about it to the people who paid his salary.

"Look Underwood, you've backed me up to a wall here, so I'm going to give it to you straight. Mr. Beringer himself has sent an ultimatum that either you straighten up or you're fired."

Zane blinked at the news. Fired. Nothing surprised him anymore.

"For Yemen or for the princess?"

"Those were just the final straws. This is about your behavior ever since you were hired by Mediacom."

"So you're going to fire me?" he said, trying to hide the edge of anger he was beginning to feel.

"I don't want it to come to that, so I've got a proposition for you."

Jack picked up a business card from the table and held it out to Zane.

"What's this?" He took it and read the name on the card.

Naomi Tyler, Image Consultant.

"She's the talented young lady who transformed Chuck Albright into the ratings-getter he is today. I want you to give her a call, set up an appointment."

"For what?"

"If you'll let her make you over into a more marketable commodity, and if you'll report the stories we assign you without veering off in your own direction, you can keep your job."

Zane's head began to buzz. Image consultants, lame story assignments, Chuck Albright's big fat toupee. It was all too much.

"You want me to get a makeover?"

"Mr. Beringer isn't comfortable with your renegade image. He'd prefer you not wear jeans and leather jackets when reporting on camera, and he'd like you to cut your hair and maybe shave a little more often."

Zane raked his fingers through hair that hadn't been cut in months and remembered that he'd also neglected to wash it for a day or two in all the chaos of getting out of the Middle East and returning to the U.S.

He'd wash his hair, but he wasn't going to cut it. Not for Gil Beringer—who'd obviously gotten a God complex while sitting around counting his billions of dollars—or for anyone else.

"Forget it," he said, standing up and flinging the white linen business card onto the table.

"If you choose to walk out without discussing this, I can't guarantee you'll have a job tomorrow."

Zane didn't respond well to ultimatums. Never had, never would.

But he also wanted to keep his job. Given the choice between saying something stupid or leaving and cooling off before he discussed this any further, he turned and headed for the door.

"Underwood, walking out is not a smart move."

"Let's talk about this tomorrow, when I've had a chance to mull over your offer."

Jack nodded. "Fair enough."

And Zane walked out the door.

PEOPLE WEARING HEADSETS bustled back and forth on the set of *Atlanta Today,* oblivious to Naomi's presence. She tried to stay out of their way and, other than one unfortunate incident involving her favorite heels and a cameraman, she thought she'd done a good job.

"Remember, you need to project a little bit of sex appeal with your respectability. Never forget you're wearing black lace under your suit."

Naomi straightened her client's collar and gave her a reassuring smile.

"Actually, I'm not," Daphne Delano said, looking confused.

"Doesn't matter. Just pretend you are."

"Right. Think respectable sex," Daphne chanted to herself. Then she paused and frowned. "I don't think I get it."

"You want to attract both male and female viewers, but you can't attract the men so much that you estrange the women."

"How do I do that?"

"Visualization techniques. You need an image to focus on that makes you feel both sexy and professional, like the lace underwear beneath your suit—that kind of thing."

She could almost see the wheels turning in Daphne's head. "Okay, I think I've got it."

Naomi had never met a person she couldn't improve.

She could size up any man or woman in a matter

of seconds, visualizing their ideal hairstyle and color, their most flattering wardrobe choices and the little cosmetic enhancements that could emphasize the good and tone down the bad. Within minutes of talking to them, she could pick out the mannerisms and speech patterns that they needed to play up or eliminate.

It was her gift.

But it was one of those gifts best shared with people who had paid to benefit from it. She'd learned at the tender age of five that telling just anyone what was wrong with them could lead to trouble.

Her grandma Anne hadn't taken kindly to Naomi informing her the mole on her chin with the hair growing out of it was detracting from her overall look, and Naomi could still remember the spanking she'd gotten for that very first makeover effort.

Daphne Delano was another story entirely. Her transformation was nearly complete, and as she sat in her place on the set of *Atlanta Today,* she'd just about attained perfection.

Her outdated mom hairdo had been highlighted and lowlighted, then styled to ultra-chic proportions. Her love of orange lipstick had been all but eliminated, and the shade of cranberry she wore now went perfectly with her dark hair and olive skin. Her big-shoulder-pad wardrobe had been replaced with a co-ordinating selection of current styles, and most importantly, her perky down-home manner and heavy Georgia drawl had been subdued to a level that appealed to the widest possible number of viewers.

She was Naomi's masterpiece, and Naomi watched with pride as Daphne went live with her new signature style shining through.

Five minutes later, Daphne finished the first segment of the show and turned to Naomi. "What did you think?"

"You were great."

"Any pointers?"

"Remember the smile we practiced. The bottoms of your upper teeth should be touching your lower lip, and keep your eyes open as wide as possible while you're smiling. No scrunching them up."

"Like this?" Daphne asked, demonstrating her version of proper smiling technique.

Her cheeks had a little chipmunk action going on.

"As you smile, focus on pulling the corners of your mouth to the side, not up."

Daphne tried again.

"Perfect! You need to practice that every day in the mirror until it becomes second nature."

Naomi went over her mental checklist. Had she forgotten to teach Daphne anything? Were there any little details that had been left out of the transformation?

As she watched Daphne interact with her cohost, she knew.

Her work was done.

She'd transformed her client from a second-rate local TV personality on the verge of losing her job to a younger, prettier talking head into the new diva of daytime talk shows. Naomi smiled as satisfaction settled in her belly.

If her sex life was a disaster, at least she could rest a little easier knowing she was really, really good at her job.

Three days had passed since she'd caught Jackson having his rendezvous with the computer, and she was feeling worse about the whole mess, not better. He hadn't called the way he'd said he would. Her only consolation was the thought of someday soon making him beg for a second chance with her, then not giving it to him.

The vibration of her cell phone from inside her bag jarred her out of her thoughts.

Naomi normally didn't keep it on while working with clients, but she must have forgotten to turn it off when she'd arrived on the set of *Atlanta Today.* She scrambled to retrieve the phone and answer it, walking off the set as she did so.

"Naomi Tyler," she answered.

"Naomi, this is Jack Hiller at Mediacom. We spoke earlier?"

"Yes, I remember. How can I help you?"

Jack had spoken with her the week before about the possibility of acting as an image consultant for

Zane Underwood, Mediacom's notorious bad-boy journalist.

No doubt an intriguing project.

Zane's face had become familiar to America in recent years as he reported live from the front lines of war-torn countries around the world. His hair was a little longer than it should have been, his beard a little too unshaven, and he usually appeared on camera in a rugged brown leather jacket that looked like it had been through one too many war zones.

Naomi hadn't understood why the network would want to change a reporter who was obviously such a hot commodity, but Hiller had been adamant that Zane's bad-boy image bothered more viewers than it pleased. He claimed the ratings proved it, and if there was anything Naomi had learned in the last few years of working with on-camera celebrities, it was that ratings were everything.

"Has Underwood contacted you?" Jack was asking, and Naomi's thoughts sprang back to the conversation at hand.

"No, not yet."

Jack sighed. "I gave him an ultimatum—he was supposed to call you or he'd face losing his job."

"Sounds like he's not too worried about finding a new one."

"Yes, well, he doesn't have a reputation for being a renegade for nothing."

"I can't make over someone who doesn't want to be changed," Naomi said, though she'd certainly love to try with a journalist who looked like Zane. As she'd talked to Jack the first time, she'd been running TV images of the sexy reporter through her head, pinpointing areas for improvement.

"I'm hoping maybe if you meet with him in person, talked to him, that you could convince him to go through with it."

"I'm willing to try."

First, there was his hair, which looked as if he chopped it off with a blunt knife whenever he got tired of its length. A trip to a good salon could have him looking like a professional within an hour.

"Let me give you his contact information...."

Naomi found a pen and paper in her bag and copied down Zane's address and phone number, then assured Jack she'd get in touch with Zane right away.

A half hour later, she'd said goodbye to Daphne Delano, and she sat in her white Cabriolet staring at the phone number and address she'd copied down.

This was her chance.

She'd struggled for the past two years to establish herself as *the* image consultant to go to in Atlanta or anywhere else on the East coast. But it was a tough business, and she'd relied on her father's political connections more than she would have liked. She'd consulted for a few well-known politicians, and she'd had some success with several local TV celebrities, yet her name still wasn't as high profile as she would have liked.

But if she could transform Zane Underwood into the smooth, polished journalist Mediacom wanted him to be, her career would be set.

On the phone, she could only be so convincing. But in person, she'd have the upper hand. She hadn't grown up in the shadow of one of the most domineering men on earth for nothing. Being Senator Atchison Tyler's daughter had taught her many things, not the least of which were the power of feminine wiles and the value of subtle persuasion.

So with the rest of her schedule for the day free, she pulled out her city map, located Zane's street and headed for his house.

April in Atlanta had its share of idyllic days with clear blue skies and low humidity, and but this was not one of them. Today was one of those prelude-to-summer days, when the damp, hot air was stifling, and there wasn't even the slightest breeze to offer relief. Naomi navigated through the midday traffic with the top up on her Cabriolet and the air-conditioning blasting.

Twenty minutes later, she'd found the historic brownstone that bore Zane's address, in the midst of the city's hippest neighborhood. His building, once a single-family home, had been converted into multiple units, and Zane's was on the third floor.

Naomi checked her appearance in the rearview

mirror and headed for the front door. She buzzed number three and waited.

"Yeah?"

"Zane, this is Naomi Tyler. Jack Hiller asked me to talk to you. Can I come up?"

Silence. And a moment later, she heard a window open from above. She took a step back and peered up at Zane. He reminded her of a soap-opera star she used to drool over in her teenage years.

Zane's dark brown hair was even more tousled than usual, as if from sleep, while his dark eyes had that squinty bedroom look that came from the day's first exposure to bright light. And he wasn't wearing a shirt.

God help her, he looked glorious without one.

She could see the delicious dip where his bicep met his shoulder, and the smooth bulges of his pecs. *Beautiful* was one of many words she could think of to describe him.

Hot, delicious and *tempting* were a few others.

He was quite possibly the most glorious sight she'd ever laid eyes on.

"So go ahead and talk," he said.

"I was hoping we could talk face-to-face, and I don't mean like this."

He looked at her long and hard, then smiled a slow smile that had probably been meant to warn her. Warn her that he was a wolf, that if she came up, he couldn't be responsible for what happened next.

Whatever. She was a big girl who could take care of herself, not some Little Red Riding Hood who couldn't tell the difference between her grandmother and a forest predator. It was just a bizarre coincidence that she was wearing a red suit. She and her fairy-tale counterpart had nothing in common but the color of their clothes. She could face up to wolves—at least the figurative kind—without flinching.

Then he disappeared from the window, and a moment later the buzzer sounded. Naomi jerked the door open while she still had the chance.

Making over Zane Underwood was the opportunity of a lifetime, and she would not—could not—waste it.

3

NAOMI TOOK THE STAIRS slowly and deliberately, careful not to wind herself, so that she could face Zane with her professionalism intact.

At the top of the staircase, Zane's door stood ajar. Naomi pushed it open and peeked inside. "Hello?"

"Jack Hiller told you I need dolling up?" Zane lay stretched out on the sofa, his lazy, sleep-softened gaze pinned on her.

"Not exactly." Her body responded to his physical presence as if she'd never seen an attractive man before. Clearly, dolling up was the last thing he needed. "Taming you might be a better way to say it."

She stepped into the apartment and closed the door. High ceilings, tall windows, hardwood floors—it was easy to see why the houses in this area were such a hot commodity. They had character like nothing that was built today. Naomi glanced around and quickly started formulating her opinion of Zane.

The apartment was a little on the spare side, but the wood floors warmed it, as did the chocolate leather sofa and chair. The room was haphazardly decorated with Middle Eastern and African art and artifacts, probably picked up while Zane was on assignment. It was no *Home and Garden* showplace, but it wasn't a bachelor-pad cliché, either.

He likely cared about the places he reported from, and a photograph on the wall of a group of scraggly children gathered around a donkey on the streets of what looked like a Third-World city suggested he probably cared about people, too.

His half-naked appearance on the couch, though, said something entirely different. Something entirely distracting.

"You think you can tame me?" he asked.

"I know I can help you keep your job," she said, skirting the sexual undertone of his question.

"So you have me sized up? Think you know what kind of guy I am based on my art collection?"

Naomi felt her cheeks grow warm. "I'm sorry— did I wake you up?" she said, making a not-so-subtle attempt to change the subject.

It was almost noon, so if she did wake him, he deserved it.

"Yeah."

"Out partying too late last night?"

He smiled, and she got a warm, fuzzy feeling in her panties. Zane Underwood had sex appeal emanating from his pores, and when he smiled… Oh, baby.

"Something like that," he finally said.

"Good thing you didn't have to appear on camera this morning."

"I'm used to sleep deprivation, but why don't we just cut to the chase? I'd like to go back to bed."

Why did a word as simple as *bed,* when spoken by this man, seem so sensual?

"I was hoping we could have lunch and discuss the possibilities I see for your career."

"I didn't realize I needed any career advice."

"Jack Hiller thinks you do."

"Jack can go screw himself."

"Shall I relay that message to him for you?" Naomi asked, hoping to call his bluff.

Instead, his lazy smile turned into a smirk. "Go right ahead, but let me revise it a bit. 'Jack Hiller, go fu—'"

"I was *joking.* Really," she said, smiling her flirtiest smile. "Have lunch with me. My treat." She sat down on the edge of the leather chair near him.

Zane yawned and stretched, appearing for a moment more like a glorious lion than a lazy reporter. "I can think of more interesting things to do with you than have lunch."

"Are you trying to scare me away? Because I've worked with Bud Callahan. I doubt you could be more obnoxious than him."

He smirked. "I could try."

Buford "Bud" Callahan was the ultra-conservative senator whose politically incorrect comments about a certain hot-button voter issue had forced him to rely on Naomi's services for his last political campaign. Her father had gotten her the job, and she'd hated almost every minute of it. Nevertheless, Bud's comments had all but been forgotten by the public and, thanks to Naomi's efforts, he was well on his way back to being embraced as a charming old curmudgeon whose views hadn't quite caught up with the times.

Zane exhaled a sigh and sat up, then stood and closed the distance between them. He was tall—at least six feet—and he moved like a man who was sure of himself, who knew what to do with his body. Naomi found herself wondering just how true that was.

Was he as good as Booty Call Ken? Would he have the talent to prove Naomi wasn't a frigid corpse in bed?

He sat down on the arm of her chair, forcing her to lean back in it. Then he bent over her, imposing on her personal space. It was just another intimidation tactic that wasn't going to work.

"How's that *crêperie* down the street?" she asked.

"I make it a rule not to eat at *crêperies,*" he said, "unless I'm in Paris and there's a pretty Parisian with me who insists on going to one."

Naomi forced a smile and called upon her rudimentary college French. *"Nous allons à la crêperie, s'il vous plaît?"*

She'd always been better at the accent than she had the grammar or vocabulary.

"Je veux faire l'amour avec toi," he said, his French quick and fluid, his accent perfect, sultry, delicious.

She barely knew enough of the language to know he'd just said something entirely inappropriate, but she wasn't quite sure what it was. Her dialogue was pretty much limited to food and transportation.

One thing was for sure, though—she couldn't back down now. Zane Underwood was going to be her next client. He may have thought he could intimidate her with sexual innuendo, but he was dead wrong.

"Has that phrase come in handy much during your travels in French-speaking countries?"

He smiled. "A time or two."

"You should put on a shirt if you plan to have lunch with me."

"I guess you won't leave me alone until I do."

"Good guess."

He lingered a moment too long, his gaze traveling from her eyes to her mouth and back again. Finally, he stood and gave her personal space back to her.

Naomi's body relaxed by a degree, and she watched him as he headed for his bedroom. The skin of his torso was smooth and rippling with taut muscle. He was thin but athletic, as if he worked out, but not too much. And the way his old Levi's hugged his hips was downright sinful.

Being here in the apartment of one of America's best-known journalists, seeing him up close and personal, having him make some unknown proposition to her in French—it was all too much.

She felt like Adam, being offered the forbidden fruit. So ripe and tempting, something she'd wanted for so very long. All she had to do was reach out and take it, sink her teeth in and find out what she'd been missing.

A rush of heat came over Naomi as Zane disappeared into his bedroom. She could follow him and take him up on his offer. It would have been the most uncharacteristic thing she'd ever done, her biggest rebellion against her morally righteous upbringing. In one fell swoop into bed, she could transform herself into the kind of woman she'd fantasized about being all those years ago at Brooklawn Academy.

But she stayed put.

For now.

Her career came first. She'd get Zane Underwood as her client, she'd turn him into whatever the network wanted him to be, and then... Then maybe she'd let him seduce her out of her panties.

Maybe.

Naomi bit her lip and smiled at the thought. But her satisfaction was short-lived, because her Tyler Moral Conscience—that inherited sense of guilt that accompanied every sin, real or imagined—could not be suppressed.

She squirmed as guilt settled in her chest, and she could feel an almighty presence glaring at her, silently berating her for having such earthly thoughts.

Naomi had learned to live her life by her own rules, but she'd never quite figured out how to get rid of the guilt.

No doubt, she was her parents' daughter through and through.

And she was going straight to hell.

ZANE COULD THINK of far more interesting things to do with Naomi Tyler than sit around eating crêpes. As he tugged on a black T-shirt and tucked it into his jeans, images of her bombarded him.

She had the sort of long, silky brown hair that reminded him of mermaids, and her brown eyes gave her face a soft, warm look that belied the tightly wound woman he sensed she really was. But tightly wound or not, her mouth had a lush, inviting quality that made him think X-rated thoughts.

There was something about her posture, though—a little too straight—and something about her smile that didn't quite reach her eyes.

What she needed was a good roll in the hay. Maybe get her perfectly coiffed hair messed up and her perfectly fashionable outfit stripped off. Then she'd relax a little and, if he was lucky, she'd forget all about his network-sanctioned makeover.

Zane tugged on a pair of leather work boots and checked his appearance in the mirror. Hair—messed up as usual. He raked his fingers through it and didn't bother with a comb. No need to impress the babe in the red suit.

Naomi.

It sounded so biblical. Maybe her parents were religious conservatives who'd raised her to save herself for her wedding night, and even then, not to enjoy her wifely duty too much. Maybe that's what her stiff posture was all about. She might have thought she was fooling him with her flirty little act, but he saw through it.

He went back into the living room and found her examining one of his journals. They were on the bookshelves for public view, but few people ever bothered to open one and look inside.

"This is amazing," she murmured as she studied a page.

Zane looked over her shoulder and saw that she was reading his notes from a trip to Kenya. He'd picked up the habit of keeping journals on his first trip abroad at the age of eighteen, and now he never went anywhere without one. He jotted down his thoughts and impressions, he sketched pictures of what he saw, and he stuck in all the photos, ticket stubs and mementos he collected along the way.

His journals helped him think through the angle he wanted to take on any given story, helped him find the truth hiding beneath all the lies.

And they were great for impressing women, too.

Naomi finally looked up at him, the journal still open in her hands. "I'm impressed."

Bingo.

He shrugged. "It's just an old habit. Gives me a good place to write down naughty phrases in foreign languages for later use."

She smiled. "I'll bet."

They walked the block to the *crêperie,* and Naomi asked questions about the neighborhood—most of which Zane couldn't answer because he was rarely home—while he tried to figure out Naomi's appeal, aside from her obvious beauty. He normally didn't go in for high-maintenance types with perfect hair, perfect clothes and perfect smiles—there were too many women in the world to waste his time with overly demanding ones—but this particular high-maintenance babe intrigued him.

When he started wondering why the hell he'd agreed to go to lunch with her, he only needed to glance down at her firm little ass in the red skirt to remember.

When they finally sat down at one of the outdoor tables, Zane decided his best tactic would be to turn all attention away from himself. "So, what's involved in being an image consultant?"

She studied the menu for a few seconds, then closed it and gave him a calculating look. "I do whatever it takes to help people realize their full potential."

"What*ever* it takes?" Okay, so when he was in the presence of a pretty woman, he had a one-track mind. That was no secret.

"Within reason, of course."

"What would it take for me to realize my full potential?"

"I can't tell you unless you agree to work with me." Her eyes sparked with a hint of teasing.

"What exactly did Jack tell you about me?"

"Just that you don't project the image the network is looking for, and that he wants me to help you."

"So I can keep my job, right?"

"Right."

"Maybe I don't want to keep it."

Naomi shrugged. "Your call."

But the problem was he did want to keep his job. He may not have approved of the network's bottom-line mentality, but it wouldn't change if he moved somewhere else. And Mediacom was one of the most respected news venues in the world.

The pay wasn't too damn bad, either.

A waiter showed up to take their order, and Zane asked for a Coke and a turkey melt. Naomi ordered a crêpe and a mineral water, and he pegged her for one of those women who couldn't eat anything containing more than a microgram of fat without going on a purging fast.

Maybe he was being a little judgmental, but her hyper-erect posture was convincing him more and more by the minute.

When they were alone again, she said, "I think you want to keep your job or you wouldn't be here right now."

"Maybe."

"And your bad-boy act is just that. An act."

"My bad-boy act?" Zane couldn't help but smile. "Is that what you call it?"

"That's what America calls it."

"I didn't realize the entire country called me anything."

"Don't play coy. You know you're in the public eye."

"Sure, I just didn't know I was on the public tongue." He smiled his most wolfish smile as he imagined the tongue action he'd like to show Naomi, and her gaze darted down to the table for a split second.

He could play the Big Bad Wolf, and with her red suit, she made a delicious Little Red Riding Hood….

The waiter brought their drinks, and she turned her attention to pouring her bottle of mineral water into a glass. Zane watched her as she tilted the glass, pouring slowly to avoid releasing too much of the carbonation.

"Are you that particular about everything?" he asked. "Or just your water?"

She smiled and looked up at him. "Everything."

"I'll bet you're hard to please in bed."

Her eyebrows shot up. "Don't you think a half hour after we've met is a little too soon to speculate?"

He shrugged. "If I'm a bad boy, I have to do something to live up to my reputation."

"I think you've done enough."

"If you think this is bad, you'd better run now before I shock your skirt off."

"How about if you stop trying to get rid of me and give me a chance?"

"I think you're more concerned about your job than I am about mine," he said.

She shrugged. "I can find clients anywhere. One person isn't going to make or break my career."

"Is that right," he said, a statement rather than a question. He didn't believe her casual act for a second.

For one thing, there wasn't anything casual about Naomi. She had the sort of polished formality that came with being a purebred Southern belle. He would have bet money she didn't even mess up her hair in bed.

And as long as she intended to stick around him, he intended to do his best to find out firsthand whether his suspicion was correct.

A girl like Naomi, though—she wasn't just going

to hop into bed at the drop of his pants. She'd need wining and dining first.

She gave him a calculating look. "I'm serious about discussing the possibilities I see for your career, but we can't have a serious discussion until you're willing to listen."

Career possibilities, makeovers, mass-market appeal. Blah, blah, blah. Whatever. Zane couldn't have cared less, so he decided he needed to shake things up a little. To keep himself awake.

"How good is your French?" he asked.

"Pretty good."

"So you know what I said to you earlier?"

I want to make love to you is what he'd said, but judging by the blank look she'd given him at the time…

"Um, yes, I've got a pretty good idea," she said.

But she didn't. That much he could tell. "Then here's the deal. You accept my proposition, and I'll agree to go along with your image consultation."

Not necessarily the makeover part, but a consultation he could handle. It would give him time to get her right where he wanted her—in his bed and out of his career business.

She smiled an uneasy smile and extended her hand to him across the table. "Okay. You've got yourself a deal."

4

NAOMI SUDDENLY WISHED she'd paid more attention in her college French classes. Had she just agreed to make out with Zane? To take off her clothes for him? To dance naked in the middle of the street with him? The only thing she could say for sure was that he hadn't asked her how to get to the train station.

And would admitting she had no idea what she'd just agreed to do cancel their deal?

Zane's expression turned wolfish again, and Naomi suddenly was feeling a little less sure of her superiority over Red Riding Hood.

"We do the consultation first," she said. "Today."

"Today? I'll need to check my schedule."

"Your schedule must be really full, what with you sleeping in till noon and all."

The waiter brought their lunch and set it on the table, but Naomi couldn't even imagine why she'd bothered to order food. She was so keyed up, eating would be difficult. She stared at her crêpe Florentine, garnished with a wedge of melon, and realized that if she didn't eat, she was going to seem like one of those women who couldn't eat in front of a man. For the sake of her image, she took a bite.

"If you want the truth, I just got back from Yemen four days ago. I still have jet lag."

"Oh." So much for her up-all-night-partying theory. "Sorry. You covered the terrorist violence there?"

"Yep, got caught right in the middle of it."

"I think I saw something about that on the news. Didn't your cameraman get shot?"

Zane nodded.

"That must have been terrifying."

"It was, and now I'll be relegated to covering weather disasters in the Midwest for the rest of my career."

"Tornado season's coming up," she said, and his expression grew darker. "But that's not what you wanted to hear."

"I just need to lay low until this whole controversy blows over."

Naomi recalled another news story she'd recently seen. "Weren't you involved in some kind of scandal over there? Something involving a princess?"

Zane gave her a look that made it clear she'd touched on an even more unwelcome subject. "Yeah, something like that."

The details of the story came to her then. "Now I remember—you slept with her, and then her daddy, the king of—"

"I'm familiar with what happened," he interrupted.

"You didn't win any image points at Mediacom for that little uproar, I'm guessing."

"No, but who knew she was a princess? Or that she was supposed to remain a virgin until her wedding night? Last time I checked we were living in the twenty-first century."

Naomi smiled. "Was she a virgin?"

"Not by any known definition of the word." He gave her a knowing look, and she couldn't help laughing.

"Well, at least you weren't the original deflowerer."

"Maybe I can reassure Mediacom with that—I didn't deflower the princess. Will that improve my image?"

"Doubtful, but *I* can. We just need to work on cleaning you up a bit."

"You make me sound like I need a bath."

"That's not what I mean."

"Why don't we just get this image consultation thing done now, and you can fulfill your end of the bargain tonight."

Naomi made like she was enjoying her crêpe. How to admit she had no idea what she'd agreed to do?

She couldn't.

With the annoying angel on her shoulder screaming, *Don't do it,* she smiled. "Okay, no sense in de-laying things, right?"

The amusement in his eyes made her feel more than a little like an idiot. "Right," he said.

Was she that obviously clueless?

She watched Zane devour his sandwich at the speed of a man accustomed to eating on the run, sur-prised that he managed to do it gracefully. Herself, she still had no appetite, but she forced herself to eat.

It was a weakness, she knew, caring so much about every little detail, caring so much that she present just the right image to the world, but hey, it was her profession. If she couldn't look her best, how could she expect her clients to trust her?

"You know," she said between bites, "after Jack called me, I went to the Mediacom Web site and watched some video clips of your news reports."

"And what's your professional assessment of my image problem?"

"For one thing, you have an attitude on camera."

"What kind of attitude?"

"Just this sort of 'I'm such a cool guy' thing."

"But I *am* such a cool guy, right?" His grin was contagious, but Naomi took her job seriously. She wouldn't be lured into joking.

"I think the attitude compromises your journalis-tic integrity to a degree. It attracts attention to you instead of the story."

Zane's eyebrows shot up, and his sandwich halted

midway to his mouth. He set it on the plate and pinned her with his gaze.

"Is that why I was nominated for a handful of major awards last year?"

"No, but it might be why you didn't win."

His expression transformed from disbelieving to pensive. "Okay, I'll watch some video clips with you, and you can show me what you're talking about."

Naomi was careful not to let this small victory show on her face. "I also think," she said, forging ahead, "that your look stands out too much."

"My look?"

"You've got this scruffy rebel thing going on. The hair, the five o'clock shadow, the jacket, the jeans—"

"So we're back to my personal hygiene again." He was clearly refusing to take this whole discussion seriously, even now.

"I mean, I think you're a little vain and like the attention your appearance gets you. But you'll never reach your full potential as a journalist as long as you're distracting viewers from the story."

He took a long drink, then fixed her with a gaze that was pure heat. "So I'm a distraction. You don't seem to be distracted from your job."

"I'm good at what I do."

"Are you good at *everything* you do?"

That was the question of the week. Naomi felt her

face flush and wished she'd been born with a darker complexion. "I try to be."

He flashed a mischievous smile, then polished off the last of his sandwich as Naomi tried not to let her thoughts stray to the issue of her possible frigidity.

And if she really was a lousy lover, would she want any other guy to know? Would she be able to summon the nerve to sleep with anyone and risk proving, once and for all, that she was lousy in bed?

Why couldn't she stop caring for one night or even a few hours? Just long enough to get laid.

"Tonight I have this thing to go to," Zane said when he'd finished chewing. "It's a party to honor shallow, self-important journalists who care more about their own images than they do their stories. Want to go?"

"I never said any of that about you."

"I elaborated on your ideas."

"You exaggerated. There's a difference." Did she want to go? She had no idea, but she figured if she wanted Zane as a client, it was one more chance to seal the deal.

"Tonight could be my opportunity to prove to you what a noble guy I am."

And it would be Naomi's chance to prove to herself she was a woman who knew how to go after what she wanted.

"Okay, I'll go. Happy?"

"Thrilled." But his tone was ambiguous. She

couldn't tell if he was simply being coy or making fun of her.

"We should watch those video clips now."

Zane shrugged and pulled out his wallet. He grabbed the check that the waiter had left on their table at some point when Naomi hadn't been paying attention, and tucked a few bills into the check holder.

As they stood up from the table, she noticed that the sun was overheating her, that she was growing sticky under her suit jacket and was dangerously close to developing big, wet underarm stains on the red wool. But if she took off the jacket, she'd reveal a stretchy camisole that she hadn't put on with the intention of it being seen by the world. It was lace, and she'd been so sure she'd wear her jacket all day, she hadn't bothered with a bra. So she had no choice but to sweat.

A lady never leaves the house without wearing a proper brassiere. That's what her mother had always said, and Naomi felt slightly scandalous to have even broken that little rule of Tyler propriety.

Somebody call the etiquette police. Next thing she knew, she'd be insisting on paying for lunch, or—gasp—wearing a white outfit in January.

"Something wrong?" Zane asked as he escorted her away from the outdoor eating area.

She waited to answer until they were out of earshot of the other customers, on the sidewalk headed to his apartment. "I'm just a little hot in this jacket," she said. "I wasn't expecting such humid weather today."

Why that was something she felt she couldn't say in front of eavesdroppers, she had no idea.

"So take it off."

"I can't. I'm a bit bare underneath." God, could this get any more embarrassing?

Yes, if the underarm stains started growing, it would.

He smiled. "When we get back to my place then, I insist you make yourself comfortable."

So much for her polished professional image. One undergarment oversight, and it was out the door. Okay, so maybe going braless wasn't exactly the method she would have chosen to advance her career, but she had a pretty good feeling it wasn't going to hurt her chances snagging Zane as a client.

And she *wanted* Zane as her client. Wanted him with some kind of crazy force that had little to do with her professionalism and everything to do with his mesmerizing appeal.

She'd do whatever it took to get him. If sex was a weapon, she wasn't above clubbing him on the head with it.

ZANE HAD TO ADMIT, he'd been slightly impressed by Naomi's assessment of him, but he wasn't about to let her know that. If he did, he'd end up looking like a thirty-three-year-old Chuck Albright, complete with shiny ties and stiff-collared shirts.

But he was even more impressed with Naomi's interpretation of business attire. She'd stripped off her jacket as soon as she'd entered his apartment, revealing a red lace camisole underneath that exposed every lush detail of two of her best features.

As he set two glasses of ice water on his desk, then pulled up an extra chair for her to sit in while they watched video clips, he could see the outline of her nipples through the camisole, could almost taste the faint saltiness of her skin that was glowing with perspiration. He was a happy man.

Thank heaven for steaming hot Georgia spring days.

He could have fired up the air-conditioning, but then that might have convinced Naomi to put her jacket back on, which would have been a damn tragedy.

Instead, he took his desktop computer out of low-power mode and opened up his Web browser, directing it to Mediacom's Web site.

"I have this stuff on tape, you know," he said. "It might be better to watch on a big screen."

Naomi shook her head. "This is easier. I can show you the clips I've already seen so you'll know what I'm talking about. Like that one," she said, pointing to a clip of a recent report from the Ivory Coast.

He clicked on the link, and they waited for it to load.

A few seconds later, he was watching himself on the computer screen reporting about recent developments in the war-torn country.

"See," Naomi said, "Right there. You're so busy doing that John Wayne impression for the camera, I almost forgot about the story you're reporting."

He clicked Pause on the video software.

"No, I don't see." But he did, sort of. He had a sneaking feeling she was right. "I'm not doing any John Wayne impression."

"Maybe not consciously, but somewhere along the way, you've developed this slightly sensational reporting style. It's the cowboy look in your eyes, the way you tilt your head, the little smirk you sometimes wear, the way you stand like you own the place you're reporting from. Watch the rest of the video and try to see what I'm talking about."

Zane clicked Play, and he watched. He'd never looked at himself through someone else's eyes before. Even with the many edits he'd done with his co-workers, he'd never really tried to imagine how anyone else saw him. Of course, no one else had ever been paid to "fix" him, as Naomi would be.

He didn't exactly like the view from her seat.

The video clip ended, and she said, "Well? Do you see what I mean?"

Zane coughed. "Not exactly."

"Let's watch another clip then." She reached for the mouse, but he put his hand over hers to stop her.

"Let's not."

Her gaze fell to his hand touching hers, and she shot him a calculating look. "Afraid of what you might see?"

"No, I'm afraid of what *you* might see." He flashed a smile, and she oh-so-casually slid her hand out from under his and placed it in her lap.

"Look, I know this can be difficult—having someone else point out all your flaws to you."

"Actually, what's difficult is sitting here with you wearing that little scrap of a top and trying to keep my mind focused on work."

Okay, it was a sleazy tactic, but if it drew attention away from him...

"I thought you'd figured out by now that trying to distract me with sexual innuendo wasn't going to work."

Damn it.

Zane shrugged and smiled. He couldn't help admiring her ability to put him in his place. "Hey, I thought I'd give it one last shot."

"Good, now can we watch another clip?"

Zane closed the browser and pivoted in his chair to face Naomi. A little bead of sweat trickled down her temple, and it was all he could do to keep from pulling her into his lap and licking it off.

"We're finished watching clips," he said. "I get your point, and while I may not agree that it distracts from the story, I see that if I change those things you pointed out, I'll be on my way to making the powers that be at Mediacom happy."

"It's really just a matter of toning yourself down. You've got a strong personality, and it shows on camera."

. "So I need to be a little more boring?"

"Not boring—transparent. You're there to report the news, not make it."

Zane blinked at her comment as it resonated through him. He was there to report the news, not make it. While he'd never set out to be the subject of the news rather than its conduit, he knew she was right. Somewhere along the way, he'd accidentally gotten his role confused. And his recent news-making incidents were a perfect example of that confusion.

"Do you understand what I mean?" she asked.

If he let her know how good she was at her job though, she'd be well on her way to turning him into someone he didn't want to be.

"Sure, you make a good point. I've done a few dumb things recently."

Okay, so that was the understatement of the day.

She brushed her hair away from her face, where it had grown damp with perspiration, and even that innocent gesture made his cock stir. He loved watching her perfect facade crumble, loved that her polish was wearing off in the heat, and that with each passing minute, she was looking more like a real woman with real desires and less like a vision of perfection.

"Then our next step is to talk about how you can eliminate your negative habits."

"You still look hot," he said. "You're welcome to strip down to your panties if it'll help you cool off some."

"But then you'd be the one overheating," she countered without missing a beat. "How about you turn up that air conditioner over there instead of trying to sweat me out of here."

He grinned. "But I like watching you sweat."

She stood up from her chair, quickly skirted his knees and headed for the door. "I think we're finished for now," she said as she tugged her jacket back on.

"Did I do something to offend you?"

She smiled a slow, sultry version of her perfect smile. "I'm not that easily offended. I just want to give you some time to think about what we've talked about. I'll see you tonight."

"Sure. And wear that top again, okay? I really like it."

"I'll hand out the fashion advice, and you stick to what you know how to do best."

That was exactly what Zane intended to do.

5

NAOMI GOT INTO HER CAR and stripped off her jacket in the stifling heat, turned the air on full blast, then checked her day planner for her next appointment. She had a manicure and facial scheduled for five o'clock, but until then, she was free. She flipped the page to her to-do list and scanned it for something that would fit into her free time.

Before she could settle on anything, her cell phone rang.

"Naomi Tyler," she answered.

"It's Talia. Where are you?"

"Just finishing up with a new client. Why?"

"Good news. I've talked to Booty Call Ken, and he's agreed to do you."

Naomi took a deep breath and sighed, unsurprised that Talia was moving ahead with her crazy idea. She glanced up at Zane's apartment. The window was empty, thank goodness. The last thing she needed was him staring down at her with that predatory gaze of his, making her feel as though he'd already eyed her as the next sheep to fall from the flock.

Even worse, he made her feel as though she wanted to fall.

"Naomi? Are you there? Can you hook up with him tonight?"

"I'm not going to need his services," she said. "I've found someone else."

"Who?" Talia demanded, sounding as if she didn't buy the story for a second.

"It's not anyone you know."

Could Naomi really have been deciding to sleep with a client?

"You'd better not be stringing me along. It wasn't easy getting Ken nailed down for you."

Yes, she could. Anything was better than sleeping with some guy named Booty Call Ken.

But Zane was more than just a booty call. He was the hottest guy she'd ever seen, and something about him called out to her in a way she'd never experienced before. She'd reacted to him like she'd never reacted to any other man in her life, and that had to mean something.

It was as if her instincts were telling her he'd play some part in her destiny, hokey as that sounded. Definitely not something she'd be repeating to Talia.

"I'm dead serious. This time tomorrow, I'll know for sure if I'm orgasm-impaired or if all my past boyfriends were clueless."

"Well, if you're sure you don't want Ken—"

"I'm sure."

"Okay, I want all the lurid details tomorrow. I've gotta go," Talia said, sounding distracted. "Bye."

Naomi hung up the phone, frowning at Talia's odd behavior.

Hell, forget Talia's behavior—how about her own? She'd somehow lost her mind since her fallout with Jackson. Lost her mind and let her brazen hussy side take over and start calling the shots.

Well, her morally uptight side had been calling the shots up until a few hours ago, and look where that had gotten her.

She glanced back down at her to-do list and spotted an item she could complete in the neighborhood of the day spa where her next appointment was scheduled. *Deliver business cards to Dad.*

Her father wanted to have extras on hand to give out to potential clients, and since he was her biggest promoter, she couldn't turn down his help. She had cards in her purse, so she headed out of Zane's parking lot toward her father's Atlanta office, where he was in town from Washington working this week.

The monotony of driving led her thoughts back to Zane, though, exactly where she didn't want them to be. He'd tested her this afternoon, left her aching and imagining and wanting in a way she never had before.

And the closer she got to her father's office, the more all her desires began to bump up against her damn moral conscience again. So she waffled back and forth, horny-guilty-horny-guilty, until she decided maybe delivering the business cards to her father was a bad idea.

Could she face him in this state? She sure as hell didn't want to. Knowing her father, he'd be able to see the guilt in her eyes.

But if she couldn't face him, then what did that say about her as an independent woman? Not much. She wasn't going to let anyone else's opinions guilt her out of doing what she had to do, and she wasn't going to let her parents intimidate her into being the version of herself they thought she should be. She lived by her own rules, not theirs.

Ten minutes later, she pulled into the parking lot of Atchison Tyler's office building and parked, took a deep breath, grabbed her jacket and tugged it on before anyone could spot her in the lace camisole.

Inside, bathed in the cool, unscented air of the office building, she started feeling more like her old self and less like her sweaty, wanton alter ego. She straightened her jacket, smoothed back her hair, and flashed a wide smile at the receptionist.

"Miss Tyler, what a nice surprise," the receptionist said when she looked up from her desk.

"Hi, Stella."

"You can go on in," she said. "He's just answering e-mail right now."

Her father's reception area was warm and inviting, from the gleaming cherry furniture to the homespun Norman Rockwell prints on the walls. Everything was meant to project the values Atchison Tyler stood for—family, community, traditionalism and America.

Naomi braced herself and knocked quickly, then opened the door when she heard her father call, "Come in."

When he saw her, his expression transformed into a wide grin, and he stood up. "Hello, sweetheart!"

"Hi, Dad," she said, trying her best not to look guilty.

She entered and closed the door, then allowed herself to be enveloped in her father's enthusiastic hug.

If his reception area advertised his public politics, his office screamed more of the same, but on a personal level. Certificates and degrees adorned the walls, along with carefully chosen family photos that her father never would have admitted were there to further his political image.

He'd even managed to make her mother's missionary work—a touchy subject if ever there was one—a symbol of his politics, with a photo of her in Venezuela proudly displayed on his bookcase.

"Now what brings me the pleasure of this visit?" he said as he settled back into his chair.

Naomi produced a small box of business cards from her purse and set them on the desk. "My cards that you asked for."

"Oh, good. How's business going?"

Naomi shrugged. If she didn't tell him about Zane, she wouldn't be able to respect herself. "Not bad. I think I've got a client who could create a lot of buzz in my favor, if I can get him to cooperate with me."

"A client who doesn't want your services?"

"It's a journalist—Zane Underwood—and this is a Mediacom-mandated consultation. They're not happy with his renegade image."

Her father made a face at the mention of Zane's name. "If you can turn that joker into a respectable journalist, I'll be impressed."

"I'm not getting my hopes up. Like I said, he's not cooperating. But I think he'll come around if his job really is at stake."

As if her father sensed there was some danger Zane posed to her, he frowned.

Naomi decided to change the subject quickly before she had to answer any difficult questions. "So have you heard from Mom lately?"

Naomi's mother had experienced what must have been a midlife crisis three years ago when she'd up and gone on mission to Venezuela. She'd claimed to have been putting her own dreams on hold for too long and, ignoring everyone's protests—most notably Naomi's father's—she'd taken off.

The frown disappeared. "Just yesterday, actually. She's helping build a school in the village."

"Oh, I think she mentioned that to me in her last letter."

Her father had mellowed over time about the subject of his wife being on the other side of the world. There was nothing he could do to bring her back, so he seemed to accept with grim approval the occasional visits they had, along with her mother's vague answers about when she planned to return to the U.S.

"She asked about you, wanted to know how you and Jackson are getting along."

This was her father's roundabout way of prying for information he actually wanted to know.

Naomi swallowed. Her father hadn't expressed any strong opinions one way or another about Jackson, which was about as close as he was likely to come to granting his approval.

"Actually," she said, "we broke up."

"Oh, sweetie, what happened?"

Now there was one conversation she absolutely was not going to have with her dad.

"Long story. We just didn't have the same priorities, and it was time for us to part ways."

The frown returned. "Well, that's actually a welcome bit of news, because Marc Atwell has been asking about you, and I think the two of you would make a fine pair."

Oh, Lord. "Dad, matchmaking is not one of your more notable skills. I can find my own dates, thanks."

He held up his hands in surrender. "Okay, okay. Just thought I'd make the suggestion. It's not every day you meet a man of such notable character as Marc."

She didn't have the heart to tell her father his noble and admirable Marc Atwell was the very same loser who'd cornered her at a political rally years ago and invited her to the public restroom for a little down-and-dirty action. He'd used much cruder terms, though.

Her father wanted to believe in the good in people and was easily angered by the bad. Naomi had learned long ago to avoid pointing out people's flaws to him.

He'd be absolutely furious if he knew what a bad girl she'd been fantasizing about being.

"I've got an appointment to make," she said, edging toward the door.

"Oh, before I forget, your mother said to keep the letters coming. They really help her keep her mood up when the going gets tough."

Sure, Naomi would be a good daughter and write. Though it took all her willpower not to ask the burning question—why did you just up and leave, Mom? And why won't you come back?

"Okay. Are you heading back to Washington soon?"

"In another week, after I take care of some business here."

She gave her father a goodbye hug and walked out the door, her shoulders straight, her posture erect. Naomi was proud of herself. She'd faced her father, and while that may not have seemed like any monumental accomplishment to the rest of the world, it was a respectable one to her.

Before long, she'd be able to do something really bold. Something wild. Something completely out of character for the good girl she'd been raised to be.

TALIA SANK ONTO THE SOFA and eyed her cordless phone, willing it to ring. She'd tried calling Ken after she'd spoken to Naomi, but there was no answer at his place. And now Talia was restless, hung up on the idea of having Ken for herself tonight, frustrated that she had no way of sealing the deal.

She'd made plans to go out with the girls, but those plans easily could be broken if it meant getting laid. Her friends would understand that a night with Booty Call Ken superceded all other engagements.

But without a cell phone or pager number, there was little she could do but hope he got her message to call. And wait.

Talia was no good at waiting. She detested it, in fact. She hadn't made partner at her law firm at the age of thirty-three by sitting around waiting for things to happen, and she certainly didn't think anything positive would come from waiting for her social life to get interesting.

She'd taken off from work early to make sure she had plenty of time to get ready for a much-needed night of fun, and if the fun wasn't going to happen on its own, she could sure as hell make it happen.

The latest issue of *Erotica Journal* lay on the coffee table, neglected, so she grabbed it and flipped through until a story caught her eye. It was about a woman whose fantasies led her to anonymous encounters in dark alleys and on elevators, in seedy motel rooms and in the back seats of cabs—wherever there was a willing male and a semiprivate place.

Talia's kind of girl, and also her kind of story.

Having just gotten out of the shower fifteen minutes ago, Talia was still dressed in her robe with nothing on underneath. She let the robe fall open as she sat leaning back on the couch, and a delicious pressure began to build between her legs as she read.

Without the promise of a night with Ken, what else could she do but get rid of some of her nervous energy?

Her hand traveled down her own abdomen to her slick, already wet center. Dipping her fingers inside, she rubbed the dampness around on her clit and began to massage.

She imagined a gorgeous stranger's cock inside her in some dark, stalled elevator, pumping into her, his hands gripping her ass, his mouth against her breasts....

And as the sweet tension built inside her, she closed her eyes, got lost in her own body—

Then the phone rang.

Talia tried to block out the sound and keep going, but a moment later, the answering machine picked up. "Hi, Talia, it's Ken. I got your message—"

She lurched across the couch and grabbed the phone. "Hi, Ken. You have awful timing."

"Oh, sorry. You're busy? I can call back."

Talia bit her lip. She hadn't slept with Ken in probably six months, but she could still remember how amazing he'd been as if it were last night. "I was just getting myself off, actually."

Silence on the line, and then, "You mean you were touching yourself."

"Mmm, hmm."

"Are you still?"

"Do you want me to be?"

She heard his breathing on the phone. And then, "Yes."

"Okay," she said.

She could do this. She'd never actually had phone sex before, though she'd done her share of talking dirty, and Talia was always game for new experiences.

She reclined back on the couch, spread her legs, and started massaging herself again. "Now I am," she said.

"Want some help?"

"You mean phone sex?" she said, smiling.

"Yeah," Ken said, his voice dropping an octave.

Was it wrong to have phone sex with the guy she'd been trying to arrange a booty call for her best friend with? Was there some unwritten rule about this kind of thing? Talia stopped mid-stroke.

Naomi had insisted she'd never be interested in Ken, so it was a nonissue, really.

Besides, Ken was sort of a public-property male…wasn't he?

Talia sighed, her state of arousal dampened by even the idea that she might somehow be betraying Naomi. "Listen, I hate to bring this up now, but I was calling to let you know that my friend changed her mind. She's not interested."

"Oh, good. Because I wasn't, either."

"Then why'd you agree to meet her?"

"I was trying to figure out some way to get an in with you, actually."

Talia smiled at the phone. This was a very interesting development. So long as by "in," he meant inside her. She didn't have the time or the inclination for anything more complex, and Ken had always seemed like the kind of guy who could understand her sex-not-love philosophy.

"By sleeping with my friend?"

"No, I was just going to talk to her, find out if you were seeing anyone."

"Wouldn't it be a hell of a lot easier to just ask me?"

He laughed. "Probably, but I was a little intimidated, and you called for your friend, not yourself."

She'd *intimidated* him? Ken, with the do-me body and the to-die-for cock, was capable of being intimidated by a woman?

The whole idea seemed both preposterous and charming.

Talia had intimidated her share of men, but usually it was with her stature—nearly six feet—or with her court record—nearly flawless.

"Why on earth would you be intimidated by me?" she purred.

"Because you're not like any other woman I've been with."

Now that was the right answer.

Talia laughed. "How can you know that when we've barely talked outside of bed?"

"It's just a feeling."

This conversation was getting slightly weird, and she wanted to get past the talking and move on to the action.

"Well, I've got a feeling about you, too," she said, smiling. "And mine's based totally on the fact that you're one of the best lays I've ever had."

"You know, I've settled down some recently. I don't sleep with everything in a skirt like I used to."

"How about girls who aren't wearing skirts?"

"Does that include you?"

"Mmm, hmm." She felt the warm, tingly tension building inside her again.

"Why don't you tell me what you *are* wearing right now."

The delicious buzzing resumed between her legs. She smiled. "Just a white satin robe, open in the front. I'm lying on the couch, and I've got my hand between my legs."

He breathed hard into the phone. "So you're naked. No bra, no panties?"

"Yeah." She was fully aroused now, so very ready to go.

She just needed him there with her. At least in

I remember that little rose tattoo you have right above your ass. That was sexy as hell."

Talia couldn't help feeling flattered that he remembered anything about her. In the great sea of women that must have been his sex life—regardless of what he claimed about "settling down"—to stand out seemed like some kind of honor.

"And I remember you've got one of the best cocks I've ever had," she said, growing breathless.

"Are you touching yourself again?" he said, his voice husky.

"I'm dipping my fingers into my pussy now," she whispered. "Imagining they're you."

He exhaled again. "I'm unzipping my jeans...."

I've got my cock out now…. I'm stroking it…. I want to push it inside you…."

Oh yeah, now he was talking.

"What position are we in?"

"You're under me while I thrust into you, playing Little Miss Innocent, your legs locked around my hips. You're so hot, so tight…. You're such a tease. You've made me wait months for this…."

Talia smiled as she stroked herself. His description was so far from the real her, she almost laughed. But how could he know otherwise, when all they'd ever done was have sex a few times?

"And now I want to make you wait," he said, "so I pull my cock out of you, and I bury my face between your legs."

"Mmm…" She could feel the tension building to the bursting point inside her as she moved closer to orgasm. "My favorite punishment."

"I thrust my tongue inside you until you're squirming and begging for me to finish you off."

"And do you?" she asked, breathless, on the verge.

"I lift you up from the bed, and you mount me. You ride my cock until we're both ready, and—"

"I'm coming," she cried.

Her inner muscles began to contract, and a wave of white-hot pleasure washed over her.

Talia could hear by Ken's own gasps that he was, too, and a few moments later, when her quaking had settled, she smiled to herself and stretched. Her body was primed and ready for whatever Ken could give her. "Why are we doing this on the phone, when we could be doing it in person?"

Ken laughed. "I don't know, you tell me."

"Give me directions to your place," Talia said, thrilled that her evening was finally going somewhere. "And I'll be there in an hour."

6

ZANE COULD THINK OF TEETH he'd rather have removed than attend the typical "aren't we great journalists" event. But having skipped out on the past
few, and being on both Gil Beringer and Jack
Hiller's shit lists, he knew Mediacom's yearly
awards ceremony tonight was a must-attend. Which
was fine, since it gave him an excuse to distract
Naomi a little more while at the same time showing
Jack what a good boy he was being by spending an
entire evening getting advice from his image consultant.

So here he was, standing outside the Ritz-Carlton,
feeling stiff in his tux and waiting for Naomi, who'd
insisted they meet at the hotel instead of riding together. He had a good hunch she was afraid of being
alone with him for too long, but she'd failed to cal-
culate that the Ritz-Carlton was full of hotel rooms,
and if Zane had his way, he'd have her naked in one
of them before the night was through.

A cab pulled up to the curb a few minutes later,
and the door opened. First came a pair of legs, long

and silky-smooth, with feet clad in glittering black heels that strapped around the ankles, then came the rest of Naomi. He took in the sight of her wearing a tight black dress shimmering with beads and felt himself grow warm around the collar. Maybe they could skip the awards ceremony and go straight to a private room—

"Hi," she said, smiling as the cab pulled away. "Sorry I'm late."

"I think I can forgive you," he said, closing the distance between them. When she was a few feet away, he extended a hand to her and pulled her closer. "If you kiss me."

She smiled and gave him a chaste peck on the cheek. "No public displays of affection. It wouldn't do a thing to improve your playboy image."

"I didn't realize I'd have to stop being a playboy, too."

"You just have to stop acting like one in public, if you want to conform to Mediacom's expectations of you."

"What's that supposed to mean?"

"No more dishonoring the virtue of princesses, no more making out with women in public, no more sex scandals, period—international or otherwise."

He sighed. "Sounds like loads of fun."

She took a step back, making the distance between them more appropriate for a Boy Scout and his Scout leader.

"Shouldn't we go in?" she asked, nodding at the glowing entrance of the hotel, where Mediacom employees and their dates were streaming in at a slow pace.

"I don't suppose I could talk you into going upstairs to a private room instead. Since you've already nixed the public displays of affection…"

Her gaze narrowed. "Jack Hiller didn't hire me to have sex with you."

He snaked his hand around her waist and pulled her closer as they walked toward the red carpet leading to the door. "He should have. Everything would be so much simpler."

"I'm beginning to think you're a hopeless case."

"Good, then maybe you'll give up this makeover crap and do what we both know we want to do."

She shot him a look. "I don't give up that easily. You may be a hopeless scoundrel inside, but I can at least dress you up like a professional on the outside."

"It's all about appearances, isn't it," Zane said as they entered the lobby.

Following the signs, they made their way to the lower-level ballroom where the event was being held.

Inside the ballroom, people stood around in small groups making chitchat. Zane groaned inwardly. This was going to be one damn long night if he couldn't talk Naomi into sneaking off somewhere and getting naked.

Getting undressed could liven up even the most miserable and boring social functions, Zane had learned long ago.

And the sight of Naomi all dressed up, looking her most polished, with her lips a perfect, glossy red, her hair draping her shoulders like satin, her skin glowing in the soft light… It was enough to make a man lose interest in everything else.

How the hell was he supposed to engage in small talk with a bunch of big-headed reporters when there was this gorgeous, prissy sex-goddess-in-the-making standing right next to him?

With his hand on the small of her back, he guided her through the crowd and straight to a table in the nearest secluded corner.

Naomi gave him a once-over. "You clean up nicely," she said. "But if you'd really like to look the part, you'll need to cut your hair."

"Could we skip the image advice for tonight? I invited you here as my date."

She smiled. "Okay, sorry. I don't normally date my clients."

"Glad you made an exception for me. Why did you?"

She glanced away from him, her gaze following a couple Zane didn't recognize as they passed by. When they were gone, she looked back at him, and he could see a spark of mischief in her eyes. "Maybe it was the heat—maybe I wasn't thinking clearly."

"Or maybe you're just attracted to me."

"Don't flatter yourself. It's unbecoming of a gentleman."

"Remember—no advice tonight. And if you think you're going to turn me into a gentleman, you've got a steep mountain to climb."

Naomi smiled. "I'll keep that in mind. And if you must know the truth, you're right, I did agree to come here because I'm attracted to you."

Her honesty almost threw him off guard. It was so out-of-character for a girl like Naomi to just come right out and state her feelings.

But Zane was the master when it came to throwing people off guard.

He leaned in close. "Then you *are* going home with me tonight, right?"

She turned to face him, confusion in her eyes. "Why would you think that?"

"Our agreement, remember? When you decided to show off your linguistic skills."

Her cheeks colored. He knew damn well she'd been hoping to forget about that whole agreement-in-French issue.

"What about our agreement?" she asked.

"I've held up my end of the bargain so far by going along with your consultation today…."

"Yes, you have," she said, her tone uncertain.

"You do realize what I asked you to do with me, right? You said you understood."

"Oh. Well, honestly, I may have fibbed a tiny bit. I mean, I have a general idea what you asked me to do."

He smiled. "You're a terrible liar."

Her blush deepened. "Okay, I lied. I don't have a clue what you said, and I couldn't even remember enough of it to look it up later in my French dictionary."

"Hmm. It probably wouldn't be very nice of me to hold you to an agreement you didn't understand."

"So long as it's not illegal, I guess my word is my word. I have to hold up my end of the bargain, right?"

"Maybe you should find out what I said before you decide that."

"Are you going to keep me in suspense any longer?"

"I said I wanted to make love to you."

The rosy color drained from her cheeks. "Oh."

"Were you thinking I'd asked you to redecorate my apartment?"

Naomi expelled a nervous laugh. "I had a feeling you'd said something a little scandalous, but I thought maybe you'd just asked me to kiss you, or… touch you, or something."

He draped one arm over the back of her chair. "'Or something' is right."

"I shouldn't have expected anything less," she said, her lighthearted tone sounding a little forced.

Zane sobered. "I wouldn't ever expect you to do something with me that you don't want to do."

She gave her chin a defiant tilt. "Who said anything about not wanting to do something with you?"

"I'm talking about not wanting to do *it* with me. There's a big difference between something and it. You can back out now, and I'll forgive you." He flashed a smile, hoping to ease the tension in her posture.

"I don't go back on my promises," she said.

"So in other words, you'll screw my brains out tonight if I ask you to?"

"Are you asking?"

"Yes."

"Then I'm saying yes," she said, all the uncertainty gone from her voice. She regarded him like a woman who knew exactly what she wanted and would stop at nothing to get it.

Again, she'd almost managed to throw him off guard, but he loved a girl who could be sure of her decisions. His blood was already pumping faster through his veins, anticipating the fun to come. There weren't many things he loved more than getting to know a woman's body for the first time, exploring her, learning what made her cry out with pleasure.

Across the room, Jack Hiller spotted them and headed in their direction. Damn, that man had lousy timing.

"Jack Hiller at two o'clock," he said.

Naomi casually glanced in Jack's direction. "I've never met him in person. We've only talked on the phone."

"Our story is, you're here on official business, as my image consultant, got it?"

She smiled. "Got it."

It was time to behave like a good boy, wipe away his smirk and exude professionalism. Definitely not time to make it clear that he was about to get naked with his image consultant.

But before Jack was within hearing range, Zane leaned toward her and whispered, "Soon as this thing's over, I'm going to take you upstairs to a nice, private suite and show you exactly why I have such a bad-boy reputation."

TALIA RANG THE DOORBELL and waited. She hadn't realized how badly she needed to get laid until she'd had her little encounter with Ken on the phone. And now, her whole body humming with anticipation, she could hardly stand still.

A light switched on inside the house. A second later, the lock on the door clicked, and it opened.

There stood Ken, his dark brown hair falling onto his forehead, his green eyes smoldering. Talia had always thought he looked like the embodiment of male sexuality, and now she remembered why. He stood a good three or four inches taller than her, his body a sculpture of smooth flesh and well-toned muscle, and she could not wait to get him hard and naked.

A slow smile started out at his mouth, and eventually reached his eyes. "Hey," he said.

"Hey, yourself. Are you going to invite me in, or should we just do it here in front of your door?"

"You've got a one-track mind, don't you?"

"When you're around I do," she said as she reached out and traced a finger along his bicep muscle.

His smile turned into a chuckle. "Come on in before we make a scene in front of the neighbors."

Talia had never been inside Ken's place before. She'd never bothered to imagine how he might live, or if he even had a life outside her bedroom. So she was a tiny bit surprised to see that his apartment looked normal, that he had furniture, art on the walls, decent decorating taste, even.

He caught her looking around. "You like it?"

"Not bad." She closed the short distance between them. "But I like you better," she said as she trailed her hands up his chest and around his neck.

Then she ended their conversation with a kiss intended to burn holes in his shoes. He responded with a little tongue action, but nothing like she'd hoped. In a matter of seconds, he broke the kiss.

"You want something to eat? I was just about to order Chinese when you called."

"Oh, um…" She was a little hungry. "Sure, if you promise we can eat in bed."

He laughed. "You're relentless."

"I know what I want—you, naked, right now," she said as she unzipped her dress in the back and shrugged it off her shoulders.

It fell to the floor, revealing her naked body beneath. She hadn't bothered with panties or a bra, knowing how easily such things got in the way. Talia stepped out of the dress and stood before him wearing nothing but a pair of black stiletto heels and a diamond belly ring.

"Whoa, babe," he said, but his gaze traveled over her body, clearly appreciative of what he saw. "I thought we could talk and have some dinner first."

"Talk?" She blinked, trying to imagine what he'd want to talk about. The pros and cons of his favorite sex positions?

He smiled. "Yeah, you know, conversation? Ever heard of it?"

"Um, sure, we can talk." It was a novel idea. "I'll tell you all about what I want to do to you after we finish talking."

He picked up her dress and helped her back into it, and for the first time Talia could remember, she felt a little ridiculous for having just gotten naked in front of a guy.

"I thought we could get to know each other."

"I fully intend for us to get to know each other—very intimately."

He took her hand and led her over to the couch,

then sat down with her. "Do you like orange chicken?"

"Sure."

He picked up the phone and dialed, then placed a delivery order as Talia tried to imagine why he was pulling this getting-to-know-you act.

When he hung up the phone, she crawled onto his lap and straddled him, aware that the position made her underwear-free state readily apparent.

"So, what sort of getting to know each other do you have in mind?"

"I've been thinking about you," he said.

Talia smiled to hide her amusement that he even had any sort of thoughts. Okay, so she'd only ever regarded him as a sex toy, and perhaps that was a bit unfair. Of course he had thoughts and feelings and furniture and such. It just hadn't ever mattered to her before. She wasn't sure she wanted it to matter now, either.

Mixing friendship with sex couldn't possibly be a good idea, and she'd learned the hard way that romance was a notion best reserved for fluffy beach novels.

"Thinking what? That you'd like to know who did my tattoo?"

He laughed. "No. Just wondering where you were, what you were doing, if you were seeing any-one…"

Whoa. This was getting weird again.

"I'm still here, still doing the same stuff, definitely not seeing anyone worth mentioning."

"I looked you up a few months ago, but I couldn't work up the nerve to call."

Talia blinked. "Why not? I'm always up for a little action."

"I guess you'd have thought I was crazy then if I asked you out on a regular date."

Um, yeah. "Maybe a little," she said with a teasing smile.

He gave her backside a little swat for punctuation. "I want to show you something."

When she didn't budge from his lap, he lifted her and set her on her feet as he stood.

"You could show me right here on the couch," she said, hoping whatever he had to show her involved taking down his pants.

He ignored her as he took her hand and led her out of the living room, down the hallway to what she had a fleeting hope would be his bedroom equipped with king-size bed. Hell, even an old futon would be acceptable at this point.

But when he switched on the light, she saw that he'd brought her to a room furnished with a love seat and an assortment of musical instruments. Okay, great. Not only was Booty Call Ken in the mood for chitchat, he was also an aspiring rock star desperate for affirmation of his talent.

Talia was interested in affirming the talent she already knew he had—for playing her body like a well-tuned instrument.

"Bet you didn't know I play in a jazz band."

She shrugged. "That's one of a million things I don't know about you."

He went to a saxophone on a stand and picked it up, then started playing it. Talia knew nothing about jazz, but she could tell he played well. "So," she said, pretending to be interested, "you're a musician by trade?"

He stopped playing and shook his head. "Just for fun. By day, I manage construction sites."

"Oh." Talia smiled, imagining all the hard-hat scenarios they could act out. "I like a man who isn't afraid to get his hands dirty."

His gaze turned dark. "I was hoping we could get past this whole sex thing tonight and talk about something else. If that's not possible, you should just tell me."

His serious tone caught her by surprise, even stung a little. She'd never felt so silly over her own sexual desires. All her life, she'd gotten whatever she wanted from men, especially when it came to sex. And now Booty Call Ken was calling her out on it?

She tried to work up some outrage, but instead, she felt bad. As though she was using him, and she deserved whatever criticism he had to dish out.

"Look, I'm sorry," she said. "I think we have a case of differing expectations here, and there's one thing I've learned from working with people. That is if you don't deliver what a person expects, there's a big chance for disappointment."

"See, I don't even know what kind of work you do." He set down the saxophone and went to her, took her hand, guiding her to the love seat on the other side of the room.

"I'm an attorney."

Snore. Who cared? *She* certainly didn't care about discussing the law tonight.

"Really, wow. What kind of law do you practice?"

"International law. Now could we talk about something besides my work?"

"Are you a jazz fan?" he asked when she sat down.

She shrugged. "Not exactly, but I don't dislike it, either."

"It's all about understanding the music. It's different from any other kind."

Talia glanced at her watch with a sinking feeling that her chance to get laid was slipping away.

Maybe she should just tell him how long it had been since she'd had Booty Cali Ken-caliber sex, and he'd understand the urgency.

"Do you have any intention of sleeping with me tonight?"

He laughed, but there wasn't any humor in it. "I guess we can't get past sex, can we?"

Another pang of guilt hit Talia. There was some vibe about Ken that she couldn't quite pinpoint. As though this was the kinder, gentler Ken.

"Okay, okay. We can, if that's what you want. I have to tell you though, I don't do serious. I don't do falling in love, and I don't do happily-ever-after. If you can accept that about me, then we can chat all damn night."

"So, what? You don't ever want to get serious with a guy?"

"Exactly!" She smiled and heaved a sigh of relief, glad he finally understood.

Talia loved her life just the way it was. She loved her sex hot, her commitments short and her freedom intact.

His gaze searched hers. "I hope I can change your mind about that."

Talia's smile vanished. "Why?"

"Because I haven't stopped thinking about you since the last time we were together. I want to give us a chance, see what might happen if we do something together besides have sex."

"Look," she said. "I'm flattered, but I really came here just to get naked."

She hadn't wanted to be so blunt, but he had forced the issue. She stood up and started across the room, feeling like a complete fool now for having come here without underwear.

Ken followed and stopped her with a hand on her arm. "You're leaving? Just like that?"

"I'm sorry, I just don't want you to hope for something that isn't going to happen." She shrugged off his grasp and headed for the door.

"I have one question," she said, turning back to him. "Why the phone sex?"

He flashed a tired smile. "I thought it might ease some of the sexual tension so we could relax and get to know each other."

"Sorry it can't work out."

She opened the door and stepped outside. He didn't try to stop her, which both relieved her and left her feeling vaguely edgy.

When Talia was alone in her car again, the breeze from the air-conditioning vent feeling uncomfortably cold, she blinked away an unwelcome dampness in her eyes.

What the hell was going on? Had the whole world gone insane, when a girl couldn't even enjoy a little no-strings-attached sex? And what had happened to Booty Call Ken, the one she'd known and lusted after?

This was so *not* how her night of fun was supposed to turn out.

7

NAOMI HAD NEVER FELT SO scandalous in her life. She'd sat through dinner and the awards ceremony unable to think of anything but what would come after. Her deal with Zane, his promise to her—it was all too much. And as the ceremony came to a close and people began vacating their seats, Zane cut short a conversation with the man next to him and turned to her.

"Let's get out of here," he said.

She smiled. "You mean there's not an after-party?"

"Just our own private one."

He extended a hand to her, and they made their way through the maze of tables toward the exit. As they passed Jack Hiller, Naomi oh-so-casually smiled and waved to him. She was being such the picture of professionalism tonight. If word ever got out what she was really doing with Zane, she'd be ruined.

Which was exactly why they shouldn't be going upstairs to a hotel suite, as he'd suggested earlier.

When they were in the lobby again, he headed toward the reception desk.

"Wait," she whispered. "I don't think staying here is a good idea."

He turned and pinned her with a gaze full of heat and promise. "Why not?"

"Someone might see us. Some of your co-workers who've drank too much probably have rooms here, and—"

"Got it, and good point. I'm supposed to stop doing things like this in public, right?"

"Come to my place."

"I'm not sure I can wait that long."

"I'm worth the wait." Or at least she could try to be.

"I'm an impatient man, but I'm damn sure you are worth it."

This was her big chance.

If she could prove that she was capable of an orgasm with a guy, then she could relax and stop worrying. And if she couldn't? No sense in negative thoughts now, not when she had Zane—her last best chance—ready to take her to bed. One way or another, Naomi was going to get hers tonight.

They left the hotel, then waited as a valet retrieved Zane's car. Naomi smiled when she saw the old black BMW pull up. It was a little rough looking, but it had style—much like Zane.

Naomi lived about twenty minutes from the hotel,

but the ride felt endless, when all she could think about was what would happen at the end of it. After she'd given him directions, Zane drove in silence as an oldies rhythm-and-blues station played on the radio.

In the silence, all her doubts started welling up, vying for her attention, chipping away at her resolve to take control of her sex life. This was her next test—to see if she could really go through with her plan.

Zane glanced over at her occasionally, and finally he spoke up.

"You look like you're in deep thought."

"I guess my guilty conscience is acting up again, telling me I shouldn't be about to sleep with a client and a man I barely know."

"You can back out any time. Don't do this if you're not sure."

"I don't want to back out. I just want to stop feeling guilty." Talia was right. She might as well have been raised by nuns, for all her outdated guilt.

Zane braked and veered off the road onto the shoulder. They were in a residential area not far from Naomi's place.

"Why are we stopping?"

Instead of answering, he leaned over the stick shift, pulled her closer, and kissed her. Naomi's insides turned liquid as his tongue coaxed her mouth open. His skin, rough against hers, was exactly the sort of friction she'd been aching for. He kissed her until she was ready to strip off her dress right there in the car, then he pulled away.

"Still feeling guilty?" he asked.

"No," she said, smiling.

"Not even a little bit?"

This time, it was her turn to lean over the stick shift. She returned his intensity with her own, slid her hand up his thigh as their tongues mingled, found his growing erection, and rubbed her palm against it until he was nearly pulling her into his lap.

When she broke the kiss, they were both breathless.

"Not even a little bit," she whispered.

He put the car back in gear, driving the remaining blocks to her apartment as if he had a fire to put out there. And after he'd parked haphazardly in the lot, he sprang out of the car and made it to her side before she could climb out.

Zane opened the door for her and pulled her out, then pinned her against the car with his body. "Once we're alone in there, I'm not going to pretend to be a gentleman anymore."

Thank God.

"Good thing, because I won't be behaving like a proper lady."

Naomi's breathing had grown shallow, and if her dress were any tighter, she was sure she'd have passed out from all the excitement. She couldn't remember the last time a guy had made her feel so hot, then she realized it was true—Zane did have a fire to put out in her apartment, and if he didn't get to it soon, she was going to burst into flames.

A few minutes later, they were in her foyer, and as she closed the door, she felt as if she were closing the door on a whole chapter of her life, as if everything that happened from this point forward would tell a new story about her that had never been told before.

She went for a switch to turn on the lights, but Zane stopped her before she could, lifted her up, and headed down the hallway. She dropped her purse on the floor, then flipped a switch as they passed one, and the hallway lights came on.

"Where's your bedroom?"

"Door on the right," she said as she slid her arms around his neck and held on. She liked this thoroughly ungentlemanly Zane—not that he'd ever been a gentleman in the first place, but knowing that he'd finally taken off the sheep suit and was parading around her apartment as the wolf he really was set her pulse racing.

He was a little bit dangerous, and she liked it.

Inside her bedroom, she'd left a lamp on in her hurry to get out the door earlier. He set her on her feet, and she fought a wave of dizziness to finally have Zane alone and ready to do her bidding.

His gaze scorched her. "You'd better take off that

dress if you want to save it," he said, and Naomi was unzipping it before he'd finished the sentence.

He stripped off his jacket and bow tie and started unbuttoning his shirt, but before he could finish, she'd let her dress fall to the floor and was there to help him. Their gazes locked as she finished undoing the last few buttons. Then he was kissing her and, somehow between the two of them, he managed to get undressed.

Naomi sighed as she slid her hands over the smooth flesh of his chest for the first time. He felt as good as he looked, and he smelled hot and citrusy. His body was flawless, his erection large and full— a promise of pleasures to come.

He bent and removed his wallet from his pants, then found a condom, tore open the wrapper, and slid it on.

She took in the sight of him again, so hot, so near, so ready, and she smiled a wicked smile.

Zane stripped her of her bra, shoes, stockings and panties, then eased her onto the bed. She lay there in the lamplight suddenly feeling a little less naughty and a little more exposed and vulnerable. Why couldn't she just relax and enjoy this for what it was—a hot night with a hot guy?

Was it because to her, tonight was so much more than just a hot encounter? Because it was the event that her sexual self-image hinged upon?

But when she looked at Zane, at his bare, delicious torso and his bedroom eyes as he climbed on top of her—hovered over her—her body hummed with anticipation. She wanted him like nothing she could ever remember having wanted before. She wanted him right down to her very core.

He brushed his fingertips along her inner thighs and sent a shudder through her. The last of her niggling doubts disappeared.

A smile played on his lips. "You want me badly, don't you?"

"Are you always so sure of yourself?"

"Pretty much, but I also like to know what you like best, so tell me."

Naomi's breath caught in her throat when he dipped his head down and placed a slow kiss on her neck. A shaky feeling erupted between her legs.

"Mmm, more of that," she whispered, plunging her fingers into his hair.

"How about if I do this?" he murmured as he tilted her chin up and placed another kiss on her mouth.

This time, he lingered, parting her lips and entering with his tongue, then taking his time as he tasted, explored and teased her.

"That's always a good move."

"Yeah?" His gaze had a knowing quality that made Naomi feel as if he could see her true desires, as if he knew she was a woman who had no idea what she really wanted.

"Yeah," she whispered.

"How about this?"

Her insides started spinning out of control as he slid his hands up her rib cage and cupped her breasts. His fingertips brushed her nipples, then squeezed them, and she sighed.

He dipped his head down and kissed the upper half of her breast, then took it into his mouth and began to suck all her inhibitions away. Whatever he wanted to do, she'd do it.

No more being a good girl, no more being proper and controlled.

Naomi was ready to go wild.

"Yes," she said in a whoosh of breath. "I definitely want more of that."

One of his hands slid down her torso, as if drawn by the throbbing ache between her legs to that very spot. His fingers brushed against her, and she heard another whoosh of breath come from her throat.

"How about this?" His hand moved to her thigh, away from the crazy ache, and she nearly growled.

Her eyes shot open. He'd freed her of her inhibitions. She reached down and put his hand back where it belonged. "I want you right there."

When he started rubbing her, she sighed.

Naomi had never been so sure of anything in her life. She just wanted to relax and enjoy the ride. *Relax,* of course, being the operative word. She wanted more than anything to get lost in the moment, to forget everything but their bodies.

Yet she was wanting it a little too much, and thinking about it way too much.

When Zane began trailing kisses up her thigh, his breath tickling her, his lips setting off little chemical reactions wherever they touched, she squirmed and buried her fingers in his hair.

And then his mouth found ground zero. He spread her legs apart, cupped her bottom in his hands, and ran his tongue over her clit in one long, slow lick that nearly drove her wild.

She bucked against him, grasped at the sheets, and sighed as his tongue dipped inside her, first a little, then a lot. He licked and sucked and explored, and she suddenly had the feeling an orgasm was going to be no problem at all.

She'd brought herself to climax alone more times than she cared to count—had become a master of masturbation, as sad a title as it was—but the thought of finally getting there with a guy… A guy as hot as Zane, no less—it was just too much excitement for one girl to handle.

"I want you inside me," she said, gasping.

And that was all the permission he needed to spread her legs wide and settle his delicious weight on top of her. His heat, his hardness, his everything felt so right, so perfect….

Naomi's head was spinning now, her mind a jumble of desires. Her body had no intention of listening to anything but "yes" and "go for it." Zane's warm breath tickled her cheek, until he nuzzled his face into her neck and started doing something amazing with his tongue.

She squirmed, and a moment later he was looking at her. His erection pressed against her, on the verge of entering her, so close, but so agonizingly not what she ached for.

"You're ready for me," he said.

"Yes."

With a thrust of his hips, he slid inside her all the way. She sighed at the way he invaded and explored her, at the sweet tension that built and built as he began to move inside her.

His gaze, still locked on her, intensified his every thrust, made her feel as if it weren't just their bodies intertwined, but also their souls. She wrapped her legs tight around his hips and tilted her pelvis to accommodate his full length, but she couldn't look away from his eyes. Not for a second.

Not until he kissed her, a soul-deep kiss that felt almost as good as he did between her legs.

He stopped and offered her a smoldering look. "I know a way I can pleasure you better," he said, removing his body from hers and pulling her up.

He sat back on his knees between her legs and lifted her hips, pulling her forward until she was against him. He supported the weight of her hips, and she held her torso up with her arms as he slid inside her again.

The new position created a warm, sweet friction in just the right spot inside her, as Zane thrust slowly into her. With one hand he began massaging her clit, and she felt her insides tensing, preparing for that ever-elusive release.

She was so close.

She closed her eyes and let go.

Let go of all the shoulds and should-nots that crowded her head. Let go of her fears. Let go of her every last thought.

He quickened the pace and increased the tension where it counted most, and she opened her eyes. Their gazes locked again as he pushed her toward a release she knew now was inevitable. And as he looked into her soul with his dark, inscrutable gaze, she felt a great rush of pleasure come over her.

Her body tensed around him, her cries drowned out all other sound, and her body quaked in an orgasm so intense she felt it all the way down to her toes. And then he spilled into her. He gasped, closed his eyes, and pleasured her with a few final thrusts that dragged out her own release as he found his.

Naomi's thoughts swirled, then formed around the idea that she'd finally done it—or Zane had finally done it. They both had. She felt like springing up on the bed and doing a victory dance.

Finally, she'd stepped out of the tepid bath and

into a bubbling hot tub, and she understood what all the fuss was about. Her body continued to quake with aftershocks, and as Zane fell on the bed and pulled her on top of him, she smiled.

There was no way she could go back now. No way she could take another tepid bath. She'd never be able to settle again for less than what he'd just given her—the absolute best damn sex of her life.

ZANE OPENED HIS EYES in the early morning light, suddenly aware of the sound of someone else's steady breathing. He blinked at the shadows of strange surroundings, for a moment disoriented. And then he remembered. Naomi, their night together, the hot sex—one encounter after another—and falling asleep with her afterward.

Wide awake now, his body warmed at the memories of what they'd done only a few hours earlier. She hadn't been as hard to please as he'd expected. Instead, she'd been so enthusiastic, so intense, Zane couldn't remember the last time he'd enjoyed a woman so thoroughly. It was almost scary how right their bodies felt together.

He rolled onto his side and found her sleeping next to him. It took all his willpower not to spoon her body to his and settle back to sleep.

But he had to decide first if he was going to stay or go. Should he wait until she woke up, or slip out now and avoid any awkward morning-after conversations? He hadn't really intended to spend the night—and she hadn't invited him—but he'd been so exhausted earlier…

Zane sat up on one elbow and watched Naomi as she slept, admired her pretty profile. And he decided. He'd leave a note, and he'd go. If he stayed, she'd get the wrong idea, and he had the sense she wasn't a one-night-stand kind of girl.

She'd want something from him he wasn't prepared to give.

He started to move from the bed, but she rolled over and moaned.

"Hmm?" she said, sounding half-asleep. "Come back to bed."

Oh, hell. He froze at the edge of the bed, agonizing again. But then she reached for him, her warm hand finding his chest, and his will to resist disappeared. He slid back under the covers.

One more time. He'd make love to her, put her back to sleep, then he'd go.

Zane grabbed a condom from the nightstand, put it on, and pulled Naomi up next to him, spooning his body against the back of hers. Then he slid his hand around her waist and up her rib cage to her breast. He toyed with her nipple until she responded by squirming against him.

"Mmm," she moaned.

His hand traveled slowly from her breast, down her belly, and between her legs. As his fingers probed her, found her wet and ready, she sighed and squirmed against him some more.

She was awake enough now for him to enter her. He took hold of her hip and pressed his cock against her, thrust inside her slowly, taking his sweet time. He ached from their earlier sex, but in a good way.

Could his body take another round of lovemaking so soon after their marathon a few hours ago? He could sure as hell give it his best try.

8

NAOMI SURVEYED THE PARK as she did her stretches, but Talia was nowhere in sight. For several years, they'd had a standing agreement with their closest girlfriends to meet up every Saturday morning at ten to jog—so long as the weather was decent—but more often than not, Talia and Naomi were the only ones to show.

Today, it looked like Naomi might be jogging solo, and jogging was the last thing she felt like doing after her night with Zane. Muscles she hadn't used since her girlhood ballet classes were crying out in offense, but still she had nervous energy to burn, and she'd been looking forward to some girl talk.

She continued to stretch and waited at their meeting spot under the oak tree for another ten minutes, then gave up and set off at a slow jog along the paved path, promising herself she'd quit after five minutes if she still didn't feel motivated.

"Naomi, wait up!" Talia's voice called from behind her.

Naomi stopped and turned to see her friend, bedecked in shades and jogging attire, running to catch up.

"Late night?" she asked when Talia had fallen in step beside her.

"Something like that."

"Sorry I missed girls' night out," Naomi lied. She couldn't have been sorry for last night if she'd tried. "But it was for a good cause."

The cause being the much-needed revitalization of her sex life.

"I missed it, too, actually," Talia said, slowing from a jog to a walk.

Naomi matched Talia's pace. "This is a new record low for us—we didn't even go a full minute."

Inevitably, their Saturday morning runs degenerated into walk-and-gossip sessions, but usually not this quickly. They could normally hold out for ten or fifteen minutes of jogging before the urge to chat set in and they gave up their charade of being athletic types.

"So what's the latest gossip?" Talia asked.

"Guess who finally called last night?"

"Not Jackson."

"I didn't get his message until today though, because I was otherwise engaged all night."

"Doing what?"

"I'll get to that later. First, tell me what this means. Jackson says he's sorry and that he wants to see me again."

"That means nothing. He screwed up, and he's groveling. So what?"

"I don't know." Naomi had been confused all morning, ever since hearing Jackson's voice on her answering machine—only minutes after Zane had walked out her door. "Should I call him back?"

"Absolutely not!"

"You're right, and after what happened last night, there shouldn't be a doubt in my mind."

"If you don't tell the whole story—"

"I want to get this Jackson thing off my mind first, then the good stuff."

She didn't want Jackson back—she was ninety percent sure of that. But the high she'd felt from her night with Zane, from going after what she wanted and getting it, disappeared when she'd heard Jackson's voice on her machine. It was as though with one measly phone call, he'd managed to wipe away all the progress she'd made.

"What did I tell you about second-guessing your decision?" Talia said.

"You're right, I don't know what's wrong with me. It's just been a crazy week, I guess, and he waited to call until after I'd given up any hope of him calling so I could tell him off again."

"It's a guy thing. Even when they're wrong, they won't call when we want them to."

Whatever. She just needed to forget about Jackson. He was a dead end.

"Okay, you're wearing your partied-too-hard-last-night shades, and you were twenty minutes late getting here—what gives?"

Talia sighed. "You wouldn't believe it if I told you."

"I would believe anything."

"I was up half the night frustrated—completely unable to sleep—because I tried to have a booty call of my own, and all the guy wanted to do was talk."

"You're right. I don't believe it. Who's the lucky boy?"

"Let's just say he's someone I absolutely do not intend to spend the night with ever again—naked or otherwise."

Naomi's curiosity was piqued. It wasn't like Talia to be coy about such matters, and if she wasn't willing to talk, that meant all attention would turn to Naomi's dirty little secret.

Talia's walking pace quickened the more they talked, and that's how Naomi knew how stressed-out her friend was. She normally wouldn't have moved so fast for anything that didn't involve sex or chocolate.

"So what did you and the mystery guy talk about all night?"

"We didn't. Once I realized I wasn't going to get laid, I left."

Naomi sighed. "Your life is so full of romance. It's really inspiring."

Talia laughed. "Spare me the sarcasm. You're

avoiding the important issue here, which is what *you* were doing last night."

Naomi was torn between wanting to spill every exhilarating detail and wanting to keep her slightly shameful behavior private. But if she didn't spill, she'd face Talia's nagging about finding herself a booty call guy.

"I met a guy, too," she finally said, a grin spreading across her face. "And we did everything but talk."

Talia stopped in her tracks, her mouth gaping open. "*You?* Had *sex* on a first date?"

"You heard it here first."

She shook her head and began walking again, her pace slower now. "I guess you were even more ready for a booty call than I thought you were."

"Stop acting so shocked. You make me sound like a prude."

"So did you come?"

"You know how to cut to the chase, that's for sure. Could you just let me tell the story at my own speed?" Naomi tried to sound annoyed, but she couldn't help smiling.

It was the most interesting story she'd had to tell in months—years, even—and she wasn't going to rush through a single detail of it. But Talia was not known for her patience.

"Okay, okay. But I want to hear about any orgasms that may have occurred *before* we make our second lap around the park."

"I'll give you a little sneak preview—I'm definitely not frigid. But speaking of second laps, we're not doing very well with our recent resolution to do more jogging and less chatting."

"Screw jogging."

"I need to go shopping for a swimsuit soon. I don't want it to be a traumatic experience."

Talia waved away her concerns. "It's all about the attitude. If you think you look beautiful, you'll carry yourself confidently, and you will look beautiful. That's all there is to it."

"Tell that to my thighs. Maybe we should meet here again tomorrow morning to make up for our transgressions today."

"If it'll make you feel better…" Talia said as they were passed by a couple of teenagers in-line skating.

"I'm not ready to reveal the identity of my Friday-night companion, either, so don't even bother asking."

Talia cast a speculative glance at her. "I remember you mentioned that journalist you were hoping to snag as a client. That gorgeous one?"

"Like you said, he's a possible *client.*"

"It's him, isn't it!"

"Didn't I just say not to bother asking?"

"Oh, you can be such a stick in the mud."

"All you need to know is, last night, I had the best sex of my life."

Talia squealed. "You had an orgasm, didn't you?"

Naomi's smile widened, but she stared straight

ahead. The news was almost too good to put into mere words. Now she understood why there were so many songs about sex.

"No. I had *many* orgasms. I could be the spokeswoman for multiple orgasms after last night."

Talia's jaw dropped, and she stared at Naomi with unabashed shock. "This is excellent news! I need details about this guy, though—the more lurid, the better."

"There's not much to tell. He's sexy and talented in bed."

"Naomi, you're a lousy liar."

"I'm not lying. For once, I really don't know that much about the guy I slept with. I guess you could say this was my first official booty call."

"Well, I'm proud of you, then."

"Sorry I couldn't meet your guy Ken last night, but now you see why."

Talia made a strange noise in her throat. "He's the guy I was with—or not with—last night."

"Wow, Booty Call Ken refused to live up to his name?"

They fell silent as they passed a couple of moms pushing jogging strollers, and Naomi realized with a pang just how far off course she'd gotten in her life from where she'd thought she'd be at her age.

Five years ago, she'd imagined she'd be the one pushing the jogging stroller, that she'd be married and have her first baby before the age of thirty. And here she was, nowhere close. Instead, she was still trying to figure out how to have both good sex and a great relationship, and so far, no luck.

"Can you believe it? He just wanted to talk. I'm completely disillusioned now."

"How bad could talking to him be? Maybe it would even make the sex more intense," she said when they'd left the moms behind.

"I'm not sticking around to find out. I crossed him out of my address book with a black marker this morning." Talia's voice had taken on a brittle edge. "Booty Call Ken has morphed into Let's Talk and Get to Know Each Other Ken, and it's a crime against horny women everywhere."

Naomi tried not to laugh. "That sounds kind of refreshing, actually."

"Right, I want to get laid and he wants to chat. That's about as refreshing as July in Georgia."

"Oh, come on. Don't you find it even a little bit charming that a guy wants to get to know the real you?"

"Not at all," Talia insisted, but Naomi had a sneaking suspicion she was putting on an act.

Years ago, before she and Talia became close friends, Talia had let her guard down with a guy, and he'd turned out to be the wrong one. She never discussed the details, but ever since, she'd slowly grown more and more callous about relationships. And the average male behavior didn't help matters.

"Well, I hope Booty Call Ken finds a nice girl who's willing to talk to him."

Talia shook her head. "It's like you and I have switched places here. I accidentally hooked up with a real date, and you've had your first booty call."

They *had* switched places, Naomi realized, and she wasn't sure she liked it at all.

ZANE SPENT SATURDAY MORNING at home, vaguely annoyed by his apartment's emptiness. He tried to focus on work, but his mind kept wandering back to Naomi. Back to their night together, and their morning, and the way she'd felt, the way she'd smelled, the way she'd sounded making love to him.

He wasn't sure he'd ever met a woman who'd needed a roll in the hay more desperately than Naomi. And he'd given it to her for all he was worth. Again and again…and again.

He'd finally left this morning after waking her up with a goodbye round of sex, making the excuse that he had work to catch up on, because the news didn't stop on weekends.

Which was true. She didn't need to know that he had this weekend off.

But he really did have work to do, damn it, and he needed to focus. Jack had left a message on his answering machine about how glad he was to see that Zane had decided to work with Naomi—ha!—

but that he wasn't going to give him any new assignments until Zane had completed his makeover and passed muster with Gil Beringer.

Jack and Gil both could stick it. Zane considered the time off his chance to pursue his own leads. He'd always chafed at being given assignments he wasn't interested in, anyway. So now, if he could get his mind on the right track, he was free to pursue any stateside story he wanted.

He opened the e-mail program on his computer and downloaded his latest messages, then read the subject lines, deleting all the penile enhancement and refinance-your-house-today ads as he went.

Nothing interesting. He skimmed the old e-mail in his in-box to see if anything required his immediate attention, and one entitled, "America needs to know," from a sender whose address he didn't recognize, caught his eye. He opened it and reread the message.

Dear Mr. Underwood,

I know you are a conscientious journalist who regards the truth as a top priority. You will be interested to learn that the highly respected Georgia senator Atchison Tyler isn't the man he has led us all to believe he is. If you dig around in his past, you'll uncover some unsavory behaviors far from befitting a man who wrote a book on moral virtues. Lies, bribery, adultery—he's not the moral compass he claims to be. Below I've included a

list of reliable sources and their contact information. I hope you'll follow the trail to the truth.

The letter was signed "A Concerned Citizen," but
Zane suspected the likely sender was one of Tyler's
political opponents. It was someone who wanted the
senator's image tarnished without having to do the
tarnishing himself, and he'd handed Zane the story
on a silver platter.

He'd received the message over a month ago, but
having been researching his Yemen story at the time,
he couldn't have been less interested in following the
trail of a domestic political scandal.

Now though, with Jack breathing down his neck
and the international scene off-limits to him, what
the hell else did Zane have to do? He'd never been
much interested in domestic politics, but the story of
a politician as high-and-mighty as Atchison Tyler
possibly being rotten at the core had its appeal.

He stared at the computer screen, mulling over his
options, and after a few seconds, he knew. He'd pursue this lead. Not only did it have the advantage of
being at least mildly interesting, but it was the kind
of ratings-grabber Mediacom loved to break. He
could get back in Jack's good graces and maybe return to doing the kind of reporting he loved.

But where to start? Zane didn't have a lot of connections in national politics. It was odd that this un-

known tipster had even thought of him as the journalist to contact, unless…

Unless they'd sent the tip to other journalists, too. The scattershot method. It was possible, because Zane could think of a dozen journalists offhand who would have been a more logical choice than him for this story.

That meant, if he wanted to be the one to break it, he'd have to act fast.

He opened a new word-processing document and began brainstorming possible people to contact, avenues to pursue, questions to ask. After fifteen minutes, he'd formed a plan of attack and decided on his first course of action.

To begin with, he needed to e-mail this anonymous person and ask for more details. Likely they'd never answer, but his motto was that it never hurt to ask. Zane clicked Reply and started typing.

He managed to focus on work for an entire hour before Naomi invaded his thoughts again, and when she did, he realized something had to give. Either he had to put her out of his mind completely, or he had to see her again.

Since they were obligated to work together for a short while, the choice was obvious. He had to see her again, sooner rather than later. Preferably today.

He picked up his phone and dialed her number. When she answered, he smiled at the sound of her voice.

"I've been thinking about you," he said.

"Zane, hi," she said, sounding a little out of breath. "You just caught me in the middle of scrubbing the bathtub."

"I want to see you today."

"Oh. You mean professionally, or personally?"

"Do you really think I'd call you begging for more of an image consultation?"

"I can always hope."

"Don't you take Saturdays off?"

"I work around my clients' schedules."

"I can't stop thinking about last night."

She sighed into the phone. "Me, either."

"So come over here."

Silence. And then she said, "The thing is, I get the feeling you're trying to distract me from my job with all this hot sex."

Zane smiled. "Is it working?"

"Sort of. But I can't meet with you unless we're meeting professionally for your image consultation."

"You mean there's more? I thought we were finished."

She laughed. "We've barely gotten started."

"I'll let you keep trying to do your job, if you'll let me keep trying to distract you from it."

"That's not much of a deal."

"It's the best you're going to get," Zane said.

"You're impossible."

He smiled. "Actually, I'm an easy guy if I'm getting what I want."

"We need to go shopping to put together your new look, and we need to schedule you a trip to the salon."

"Forget the salon."

"Zane, you've got to do something with your hair."

"I've already got a guy who cuts it for me."

"With a dull knife? I'm not doing my job unless I take you to a good stylist. It's part of the deal."

Zane exhaled. Jack Hiller would be expecting him to clean up some, and Zane knew his hair was part of the problem. "Fine, but if I walk out of there looking like a helmet head—"

"Give me a little credit. I make people look better for a living, not worse. And for the record, I like your hair. I just think it needs a good cut and style."

"No hair spray."

"Okay, no hair spray. Do we have a deal?"

"Yeah, I've got some free time on Monday if you can get me an appointment anywhere then."

"That's kind of short notice, but I'll see what I can do."

"That still doesn't help me out with the problem I'm having right now," he said, leaning back in his chair and staring up at the ceiling.

Nothing but Naomi naked in his arms was going to help him with his immediate problem.

"We need to address the issue of your wardrobe, which seems to consist of nothing but black T-shirts and jeans."

"So what's the problem?"

"And that leather jacket you like to wear on camera—doesn't that get hot in Africa?"

"Yeah, but it looks cool."

"It has its charm, but it also looks like it's been rolled over by a few Humvees."

Zane laughed. "I think it has, actually."

"It's gotta go. Meet me at Brooks Brothers at the mall near your place, and we'll put together a new look for you."

"Why can't I just keep my own look and spiff it up a little?" he said, his hopes of getting laid tonight fading fast.

"We'll try to do that. But you need a wardrobe overhaul."

"Not at Brooks Brothers. I'll look like a cookie-cutter reporter fresh out of journalism school."

"Would you stop protesting every little suggestion I have and give me a chance? It's a good store for picking up a few basic items. Then we can expand out from there."

Zane didn't have an ounce of faith that he'd turn out looking anything like himself if he let Naomi have her way with him, but he didn't have much choice at the moment. The desire to get Naomi into bed again was enough to risk getting decked out in a stiff oxford and maybe even a shiny striped tie.

"Okay, okay. I'll meet you at the mall. What time?"

Over the phone, he could hear her flipping through pages. She probably had her Saturday planned out by the hour, complete with number of minutes allotted for weekend relaxation.

"I can be there at four o'clock."

"Let me check my schedule," Zane said, smiling to himself as he flipped through his blank calendar that he never could be bothered to write things down on. "Looks like I'm free."

After they'd said goodbye, he hung up the phone and stared at his computer, trying to figure out where the uneasy feeling in his gut had come from. Was it Naomi? The story? His impending makeover?

It had to be the makeover. He didn't like being shaped and molded into someone he wasn't, especially not by his employer. There had to be another way.

But until he found it, he fully intended to enjoy his hot little image consultant for all she was worth.

9

NAOMI GLANCED AT HER WATCH and heaved a sigh of exasperation. She looked around the Brooks Brothers store again, but Zane was nowhere in sight. She'd already set aside a dressing room for him and filled it with the clothes that would make up the base of his ideal career wardrobe, but he was almost an hour late for their meeting.

She dug around in her bag until she found Zane's contact information, then punched his home number into her cell phone. No answer. She tried his cell phone next, and he answered after two rings.

"Did you forget our appointment?" she asked by way of greeting.

"Hello to you, too."

"I've been waiting for you for the past hour."

"Oh, sorry," he said, not sounding the least bit apologetic. "Didn't you get my message?"

"No."

"I had some work come up that I couldn't blow off. I called and got your machine."

"I wouldn't have gotten it. I've been out all afternoon."

"Sorry. I didn't think to call your cell phone."

Naomi's temper flared. She would not be toyed with by some playboy journalist with a bad attitude. Even if he was amazing in bed.

"If this is your way of getting out of our agreement, you can forget about it. I want you here in fifteen minutes."

He laughed. "I'm sorry. I can't blow off my other appointment just to play dress-up with you."

"You're wasting my time. Is this other appointment of yours important enough to lose your job over? Because I can call Jack Hiller right now and let him know you're refusing to cooperate."

Silence.

"If you're not here in fifteen minutes, I'm calling him."

"You wouldn't."

"Do you really want to test me on this?"

He muttered a curse, then breathed into the phone. In the background, Naomi heard a horn honk.

"I need a few minutes to make a phone call," he finally said, sounding none too pleased. "And I'm on the other side of town. I'll need twenty minutes to get there."

"Fine. I'll give you thirty," she said, then hung up the phone.

Okay, so maybe she'd turned into psycho bitch.

Maybe she'd overreacted a tiny bit, but she would not have her time wasted.

Naomi dropped her phone into her purse and expelled a pent-up breath, blinking away an unexpected dampness in her eyes. Here she was, the cheerleader who'd just been dumped by the star quarterback. And she'd just had to beg him to come back. At least that's how she felt.

No, that was ridiculous.

She was freaking out because her professional reputation was on the line, and she didn't want her biggest client ever skipping out before she'd even gotten a chance to improve him.

The fact that they'd slept together no doubt complicated matters, though—and complicated her emotions as well. She might not have reacted so strongly to any other client blowing her off, and this was yet another example of why she shouldn't be sleeping with Zane.

But the thought of their night together, of the myriad ways he'd pleasured her, of the tingly sense of satisfaction she felt…

It was complicated.

She didn't want to give up the best sex she'd ever had as soon as she started having it. But she also didn't want to blow her chance to make over Zane and set her career on the fast track to success.

Too damn complicated.

Naomi arranged with the salesclerk for Zane's

dressing room to remain reserved until she returned with him, and then she set out across the mall to the coffee shop she'd eyed on the way in. If ever her nerves needed the soothing effects of caffeine, it was now.

Ten minutes later, with cafe latte to go in hand, she stood in front of Victoria's Secret, eyeing a little black lace ensemble that she couldn't help but imagine wearing for her next encounter with Zane.

And there she was—already assuming there'd be a next encounter. Not even letting her own good sense talk her out of it. Assuming, even, that after the way she'd just behaved on the phone, Zane would ever want to sleep with her again.

Instead of reality dissuading her, she simply shrugged it off. She was the same woman who'd tossed her ex's clothes out the window, after all. She could handle Zane.

And there had been his mention of trying to distract her from her job. She'd let herself be distracted a little, if it was the right kind of distraction—and with Zane, no doubt it would be.

So she marched into the store without feeling the least bit embarrassed, picked out her size and carried the bra and thong panties to the register. After she'd bought it, she tucked the bag into her purse, intending to return to Brooks Brothers to wait for Zane, but instead she found herself on her way to the public restroom to change.

If Zane wanted to give her a distraction, she might as well dress for it. She went into the ladies' room and changed out of her nice-but-boring underwear and into the new bra and panties that put her in exactly the right mindset for seduction. Zane could believe he was distracting her from her job all he wanted, but she knew the truth. She was simply getting what she wanted—and she'd do her job, regardless of what he thought.

A few minutes later, she was dressed again, and she went out into the mall. She found a bench outside the store, and she sat on it, sipping her coffee until Zane showed up.

He eyed her darkly as he stopped in front of her. "Is that how you treat all your clients?"

"Only the uncooperative ones," she said as she stood.

Naomi tossed her coffee cup into a nearby garbage can, then followed Zane into the store. If she had to read his posture, she'd say it was screaming, "Pissed off."

The salesclerk, a guy in his twenties who looked like the poster boy for Brooks Brothers, approached them. "May I show you to your dressing room now?" he asked.

"Yes, please."

Zane cast a wary glance at her but said nothing as he followed them to the dressing area and into a small room equipped with mirrors, a clothes rack and a cushioned bench.

"Just let me know if you require any other items or sizes. I'll be right outside," the salesclerk said, then closed the door.

Naomi sat on the bench, suddenly aware that she was alone with Zane, and that he was about to get naked. She normally would have waited outside for clients to try on clothes, but since she'd already seen him in the buff once…

"While I was waiting for you, I went ahead and picked out some clothes I thought would suit you well on camera."

He eyed the assortment of conservative garments hanging from the rack but reserved comment.

Face-to-face, alone with him, the memory of their night together so fresh in her mind, Naomi realized the last thing she wanted to do was fight with Zane.

"Can we call a truce?" she said in her best sugar-sweet southern drawl.

"Why the sudden change of heart? Don't you want to threaten me and badger me a little more?"

"I'm sorry I took such a nasty tone. I don't think we can work productively together if there are hostile feelings."

He cast a skeptical look at her. "You've got that right."

"Will you accept my apology?"

"Sure. I guess I owe you one, too, for blowing off our appointment." He smiled then—a slow devil's smile.

Naomi crossed her legs and tried to ignore the sweet buzzing that was starting up between them. She nodded at the rack of clothes. "If those styles don't work for you, we can always try something else. I'd just like to start out with these basic pieces as we go over the principles for building a career wardrobe."

He crossed the dressing room and stopped a few inches from her, then took her hand and pulled her to her feet. "I didn't realize getting dressed could be so damn complicated."

She smiled, his nearness an entirely distracting reality. "Not complicated, just not something that most people know instinctively."

"Oh yeah?" His smile turned predatory. "Want to talk about what I *do* know instinctively?"

Oh yes, she certainly did. But first, work. "We'd better stay focused on the task at hand," she said, her voice unexpectedly tight. "For now," her inner bad girl added, visions of hot sex already dancing in her head.

His nearness was muddying her thoughts, so she stepped aside, then went to the rack of clothes and pulled out a pair of flat-front khakis and a white oxford.

"I had to make some assumptions about your size, so hopefully these will fit. Let's start out by trying them on."

Zane kept his gaze locked on her instead of the

clothes as he removed his shirt, shoes and pants, then stood before her naked except for a pair of snug white briefs.

She dared to look him over and saw that he was growing erect. Oh Lord, the things she ached to do right now…

In a matter of seconds, he was fully erect. "Damn," he said, glancing down at his own crotch. "Trying on clothes might be a little painful at the moment."

She couldn't help laughing. "Is this some kind of distraction technique?"

"Honey, I don't exactly control when things happen down there."

"Well, then, you'll just have to do your best to try the clothes on," she said, but she didn't even sound convincing to her own ears.

What she wanted to say was that she'd be perfectly happy to relieve him of his not-so-little problem.

He came to her, took the clothes from her hands, and tossed them to the floor. "You sure about that?"

Hell no.

"Um…" She didn't get a chance to make up any lame response because he silenced her with a kiss.

As his tongue coaxed her mouth open and began demanding her attention, he pulled her body against his, and she felt the full extent of his problem. Oh yes, she'd definitely need to help him with that. He pushed his hands beneath her top and found her breasts, aching, with nipples erect. He massaged and teased them, then pushed her bra down and palmed her bare flesh until she was gasping for more.

He broke the kiss and regarded her with eyes darkened by desire. "You didn't expect last night to be a one-time performance, did you?"

Without waiting for a response, he tilted her head back and found her neck with his mouth, where he began sucking, teasing, biting gently.

"Umm…" she said, more of a moan than a response. "I…hoped not."

Naomi clung to him, her greedy hands expl… the smooth, hard flesh of his back, her mind danc… ing over fantasy images of their bodies locked together in sex.

Here in the dressing room, in the mall parking lot—wherever, whenever, she was so very ready for it.

She licked his shoulder, nipped at his flesh, holding on for dear life as he made his way from her neck to her ear.

He pushed her skirt up to her waist and pushed her panties aside. His fingers spread her lips apart as he teased her, aroused her…. Then he dipped inside her, and she cried out.

"Shh," he whispered, a teasing smile playing on his lips. "That salesguy might think we're calling for another size."

"Mmm," she moaned softly.

His fingers plunged deeper inside her. "I want to bury my cock inside you," he whispered, his words a raw shock to her system.

She went from burning to on fire in an instant. Naomi unzipped her skirt and let it fall to the floor, then stripped off her top and panties as he helped her out of her bra.

So much for her fancy underwear. He'd barely gotten a glimpse of them. But they'd served their purpose, having given her the confidence to go after what she wanted. Zane had set her on the course of becoming a woman with a great sex life, and she wouldn't turn back now.

He tried to turn her around, but she stopped him. "Not so fast. I think you need professional help," she said as she slipped her hand inside his briefs.

He sighed. "I didn't realize that was on your list of services."

"Not for my regular clients, but for a hard case like you, I can make an exception," she said with a naughty little smile.

She tugged his briefs down, and he stepped out of them as she sat on the bench. Then she pulled him between her legs and took his erection into her hand again. She'd tasted him last night, felt the power of having him in her mouth, but it hadn't lasted nearly long enough. He'd been impatient for more, and so had she.

This time, she intended to savor him.

Naomi took him into her mouth and ran her tongue along his length, thrilling at the gasp he expelled. He buried his hands in her hair as she teased the head of his cock with her tongue. And the more she teased, the more tension she could feel coiling inside him.

She ran her fingernails up his inner thigh and across his balls, then cupped them as she continued to suck. She started building up a momentum, and then someone knocked on the door.

"Is everything okay in there?" It was the salesclerk.

Naomi froze and looked up at Zane. His eyes shot open.

"We're doing just fine, thanks!" he called out.

"Okay, just let me know if you need anything."

"Will do," Zane said in a voice edged with tension.

Naomi tried to pick up where she'd left off, but he grasped her by the arms and lifted her up, then covered her mouth with a hungry kiss.

"I want you *now*," he whispered when he broke the kiss. "Before we have any more damn interruptions."

Then he turned her around and propped one of her legs on the bench as he gripped her hips. She bent forward to accommodate him, resting her arms against the wall as a delicious swirling began between her legs. He pressed against her wet opening, and it took all her willpower not to cry out in frustration. She wanted him pumping inside her, easing the crazy ache in her, driving her toward a release that was building with his each and every touch.

And then he was gone for a moment, searching for his wallet. She heard the crinkle of a condom wrapper, smelled the scent of rubber, and felt him against her again.

Without hesitating, he held her hips firmly and pushed inside her all the way.

Naomi sighed, closed her eyes and braced herself against the wall as he thrust into her—each thrust more purposeful than the last, each pushing her toward a release she had little doubt she'd find.

As he stroked her breast with one hand, his other hand dipped between her legs and massaged. He was an expert on the subject of her body after only one night. He knew where to touch, and when, how much pressure to apply, when to let up and when to drive her over the edge.

She heard herself gasping but was helpless to control it, couldn't have cared less if the salesguy came barging in to see what was going on, and a moment later, she felt a dam release within her. Waves of pleasure came bursting forth, convulsing her as Zane pounded into her, and then she heard the gasps of his orgasm, too.

His final few thrusts came on the heels of her release, drawing it out, causing her inner muscles to continue contracting around him as she tried to catch her breath.

They remained locked together for a few moments after, the room silent as they recovered. Then he withdrew from her, turned her around, lifted her up and pinned her against the wall. She wrapped her legs around him and kissed him again and again, grateful and satisfied, yet hungry for more.

"Let's get out of here," he whispered.

Her sentiments exactly. But not before they'd done what they came here for. "Absolutely. After you try on these clothes," she said.

Zane's gaze darkened again, but a smile played on his lips. "You're relentless."

"Just trying to do my job."

"What if I just keep you like this until you forget about this makeover thing?"

She smiled. "You'll get tired soon, and you'll have to put me down."

"You're right," he said as he stepped away from the wall and set her back on her feet. "You're heavier than you look."

Naomi grabbed her panties from the floor and tugged them on. "You can start with the white oxford and the black pants."

Zane made a growling sound, but he didn't protest anymore. He may have thought he was distracting Naomi, but he was sadly mistaken. If she kept him satisfied sexually, he'd keep right on doing whatever she asked.

"WANT TO GRAB SOMETHING to eat?" Zane asked as they passed a chain restaurant near the mall entrance.

"Yeah, all that shopping and trying on clothes has made me hungry. The Mexican place at the north entrance of the mall is good."

He was hungry, too, but more for her than for food. He'd never met a woman he couldn't get enough of, but after twenty-four hours of a sexual frenzy with Naomi, he could hardly call himself sated. Maybe if they spent all night tonight doing what they'd done all night last night, he'd be feeling a little more balanced in the morning.

After three men's clothing stores and two upscale department stores, Zane's hands were weighed down with shopping bags, and he was pretty sure his credit card had a hole burned in it. Not to mention that after two sexual encounters in two different dressing rooms, he should have felt spent physically, too.

But he was nowhere close.

He was, however, damn sure he'd just bought a bunch of clothes he never would have picked out himself.

But he'd seen again how good Naomi was at her job. She might have selected clothes he wouldn't have, but she'd found things that looked good on him, that were stylish but classic, and that didn't make him want to run naked from the dressing room.

If he had to change his style to suit Mediacom, he couldn't say he was dissatisfied with the style Naomi had picked out for him. Not that he wanted someone else choosing his clothes for him, but in the great scheme of things, it really wasn't all that big a deal.

They headed toward the Mexican restaurant, and he had the odd sensation of being out shopping with a girlfriend. Not that he'd had a steady one of those in a while, but he'd had more than his share of the short-term variety.

Naomi should have felt like neither. She was shorter than short-term, a pretty little high-maintenance diversion that he had no intention of sharing more than his bed and his image overhaul with.

But…

She was more than her polished appearance let on. She was smart, funny and surprisingly in control, even when she was pretending not to be.

Like today, for instance. While he'd tried to distract her, she'd somehow turned the whole thing around and used sex as her way of luring him from one store to the next, from one dressing room to the next. He couldn't help but admire the brilliance of her tactics, even as he was being sucked in by them.

They passed by a bookstore, and he saw Naomi turning her head to read the titles in the window.

"Want to go in?" he asked, curious to see if she would go straight to the self-help aisle, or to the fashion magazines. He had her pegged as one of those women who read nothing but books with titles like *The Ten Habits of Highly Anal-Retentive People*, but his brief encounter with her apartment last night and this morning neither confirmed nor denied his suspicion. He'd caught a glimpse of a *Vogue* magazine on her coffee table on his way out the door, but other than that detail, he'd been too tired to notice anything.

But she surprised him again by browsing the general fiction on the table at the front of the store. He went to the biography section and grabbed a new release at the end of the aisle, then pretended to flip through it while watching her from the corner of his eye.

Why the hell did he even care what she read, anyway? But he knew. He wanted to finally be right about some aspect of her personality. He wanted her to have some big, obnoxious flaw he couldn't stand. If she wasn't a self-help fanatic, then he at least wanted her to be the type who got all teary-eyed over amazing pet rescues or something like that.

Okay, so her outburst over his being late for their shopping excursion today might be considered slightly obnoxious, but really, he'd had it coming. He could have scheduled the meeting with a source he'd contacted on the Atchison Tyler story for another time, but he'd deemed it more important than shopping for polo shirts.

After Naomi read the back cover copy of a few books at the fiction table, she wandered to the half-off table near where he was standing and picked up one of his favorite humor titles. When she started flipping through the book, giggling every few pages, he muttered a curse and put the biography down.

He walked over to the table and started halfheartedly browsing the books. "So, do you ever read self-help books?"

She shrugged. "No, I like to be the one giving the advice."

"How about cozy quilting mysteries? Or amazing pet-rescue tales?"

She looked at him like he'd just made quacking sounds.

"No, and no," she said. "Are you okay?"

So much for that theory.

"I probably should eat soon," he lied. "My blood sugar drops and I start talking like a lunatic."

"Let's go, then," she said, looking at him curiously as they picked up their bags and left the store.

And as they headed for the restaurant, Zane battled a growing unsteady feeling that had nothing to do with low blood sugar—and everything to do with the fact that Naomi was throwing him utterly and completely off balance.

10

TALIA SHUT DOWN her computer, determined not to work on a Saturday night. With last night's planned fun having turned into a get-to-know-your-booty-call date, she fully intended to make up for it by having twice as much fun tonight. Nightclubs, here she came.

She pushed away from her desk and headed to her bedroom to change.

She'd just shimmied into her favorite black club dress and was applying Kiss Me Red lipstick when the doorbell rang.

Great, someone with something to sell on a Saturday night. She continued her lipstick application, with no intention of answering. But once her makeup was done, the doorbell rang again.

Okay, so she'd have to tell the person more clearly to get lost. She went to the front door, jerked it open and found herself face-to-face with Ken. He held a bouquet of pink roses—her favorite. How the hell had he known that?

He was wearing a sage-green polo that accented

his green eyes, and a pair of faded jeans that beautifully accented his package. He looked amazing, and if she hadn't known he was the same Ken who'd ruined her night, she would have dragged him inside without a second thought.

"What are you doing here?" she blurted, realizing a second too late that it wasn't the nicest response to a guy showing up at her door bearing flowers.

"Hi to you, too." His gaze traveled down her body and back up, clearly appreciative of what he saw.

This wasn't her favorite club dress for nothing.

"Sorry. What I meant to say is 'hello.' I thought you were some kid trying to sell me overpriced magazine subscriptions."

"Can I come in?" he asked.

"I was just about to head out for the evening, but I've got a few minutes."

"I was hoping I'd catch you before you went anywhere." He stepped inside and handed her the flowers.

"Thank you. What's the occasion?"

"You're the occasion."

Talia blinked. Could this whole Ken thing get any odder? Next he'd be telling her he'd given up casual sex.

"What's that supposed to mean?"

"I came to give you what you want," he said, and Talia wondered if it would be too forward to strip her panties off right then and there.

Instead, she smiled. "Now you're talking about something I want to hear," she said as she dropped the roses onto the coffee table and closed the distance between them.

"You haven't heard my condition yet," he said, and Talia stopped, inches from him, inches from getting laid.

"Oh?"

"Here's the deal. I'll do whatever you want tonight in bed, if you'll do whatever I want tomorrow night outside of bed—on a real date."

"A…real date. As in dinner and a movie, stuff like that?"

"Yeah. Stuff like that. We get to know each other, see if we're compatible. You give me a real chance."

"Oh." She felt like she was becoming a broken record, but she couldn't think what else to say. Ken had ignored all booty-call etiquette. Talia wasn't sure she'd ever be able to trust a sex-only relationship again. "It's like I said before, I'm really not a let's-go-steady kind of girl."

And she probably never would be. She liked her life just the way it was. Simple, career-focused, unencumbered by love. She'd tried the serious-relationship thing, and it had made her miserable. She didn't want to go there again—especially not with a guy known to all her friends as strictly booty-call material.

He smiled. "That's because you haven't given the right guy a chance yet."

"There is no right guy. Trust me, I've looked, and I've been completely unimpressed by the selection. No offense," she added, feeling like a bitch now. "I have impossible standards."

Looking undeterred, Ken shrugged. "All I'm asking for is one date. Give me a chance, and if you're not interested after our date, I'll never bother you again."

His offer was tempting. She could do one date, certainly, if it meant a night of hot sex. And she did have a heart. Having a cute guy show up on her doorstep bearing roses and asking her out on a date was just so nauseatingly sweet and old-fashioned....

Okay, so he'd actually proposed a sex-for-dating trade, but still, he'd brought flowers—her favorites, even—and she couldn't remember the last time a guy had done that.

"What made you bring pink roses?" she asked.

"I remember seeing some of them on your table when I was here last fall, so I saw these, and they reminded me of you."

Again, she was speechless. Was he for real?

"You like them?" he asked.

"Of course."

"So, what do you think?"

"I think I like your offer. I just don't want you to get your hopes up—"

He smiled and pulled her against him, then silenced her with a kiss that likely melted her toenail polish. *This* was the Ken she remembered—the one she wanted to spend the night with.

She led him over to the couch, grabbed the stereo remote and queued up her favorite make-out CD—a compilation of Barry White's greatest hits—then pulled her dress off over her head and tossed it on the floor.

Ken's gaze traveled over her, from her pink satin-and-lace bra to her matching panties, then back up.

"Come here and let me taste you," he said as he hooked a thumb in the side of her panties.

He slid them down her legs, and she stepped out of them, kicking them aside, her insides humming to find out what kind of tasting he had in mind. When he reclined on the couch and pulled her on top, urging her forward until she was straddling his face, her girl parts did an imaginary victory dance.

"Closer," he said, tugging her hips down, and that was all the instruction she needed.

When his mouth came in contact with her pussy, she sighed, closed her eyes, and let her head fall back. His tongue traced her lips, then caressed her clit, and finally thrust into her. His pace was deliciously slow, and for once, Talia was fine with letting him take his time.

If this was going to be her last night of sex with Ken—and surely it was with him getting all clingy on her—she wanted to savor every delicious moment of it. Commit it to memory, because there weren't many lays out there as good as Ken.

What was the likelihood she'd even find another one in her lifetime?

She didn't have to ruin her fun with worrying because he started working her clit in a steady rhythm that obliterated all thought. Talia's breathing grew fast and shallow, and she rocked her hips against his face.

Then he plunged his fingers into her, probing her most sensitive spots, working her fast toward an orgasm that she couldn't have slowed down if she'd wanted to. When he found her G-spot with his thumb, and it was all over.

In only minutes since he'd arrived at her door, waves of pleasure swept through her. Talia bucked and cried out, gasped, moaned, lost all sense of time and place. And Ken, in his amazing expertise, knew all the right touches and tongue moves to keep her riding the wave of her orgasm long past when it would have ended with any mortal guy.

Minutes later, when she was resting on his chest and had caught her breath, she realized that was exactly what she'd been missing recently. Really great sex. She'd had good sex, decent sex, okay sex—but none like what Ken could deliver.

She placed a long, deep kiss on his mouth, then started stripping him of his clothes before he could change his mind and decide he wanted to play twenty questions. When she was tugging off his underwear, she looked up at him and smiled, her heart going pitter-patter at the sight of his long, hard cock.

"Condoms are in the candy dish," she said. "Can you grab one?"

He glanced over at the end table and grinned. "Who needs candy when you're around to eat, right?"

"My thoughts exactly."

He plucked a condom from the dish and handed it to her, likely having remembered her talent for putting them on creatively. She tore the wrapper open with her teeth and withdrew the condom, then placed the tip of it between her lips. Her whole body humming with anticipation, she put her mouth against him and slid the condom down the length of him.

As he sat up, leaning back against the sofa, she climbed on his lap and pressed herself against his cock.

"You've got an amazing body," he said, taking her breasts in his hands.

"So do you."

She loved that his hands were big enough to cover her breasts, that his body was big enough to make her feel feminine, even kind of petite—and there weren't many men out there who could do that.

Talia tossed her hair over her shoulder, arched her back and mounted his cock. He slid inside, fill-ing her and easing her deepest ache. As she began rocking her hips, Ken closed his eyes and sighed. For the first time, she saw something vulnerable about his face, something entirely human.

And she realized he wasn't a sex god, or a bedroom superhero, or any sort of supernatural hottie. He was just a guy, with feelings, emotions, opinions—all that stuff that came with being human. And she'd been treating him like anything but.

He cupped her ass with his hands and set the pace, slow and steady. Then his fingers began exploring, working their magic again, and the troubling thoughts disappeared.

One unforgettable night with Ken—that's all Talia wanted. She'd let nothing stand in her way of having it.

ZANE WATCHED NAOMI as she lay next to him, looking around his bedroom. She was probably deciding what color he should paint the walls. He'd already figured out that she saw everything, critiqued everything and had an opinion on how to improve everything. It should have been annoying, but he actually kind of liked her confidence.

"You need a few more lamps in here," she said, proving his theory.

"Thanks for the tip." He grinned. "Do you want something to drink?"

"No, thanks."

Good, because he wasn't sure if his leg muscles could hold him up for a walk across the room, let alone a trek all the way to the kitchen. It was after midnight, and they'd spent the evening continuing what they'd started in the dressing rooms at the mall.

He could say for sure now that he was spent. At least for tonight. After a good night's rest though…

He pulled Naomi closer, pressing himself against her backside. He may have been too exhausted for any more action at the moment, but still, the contact of her warm flesh caused him to stir.

He traced her belly button with his fingertip as he nuzzled his face against her hair.

"How did you get so damn sexy?" he said.

She laughed. "Don't let my parents hear you say that. They raised me to be a proper lady. Nothing like I've been behaving with you."

"Oh yeah? Would your dad chase me off with a shotgun if he knew what we were doing?"

"He's a little more subtle than that. He'd probably force you to read his book about moral virtues, then lecture you on all the reasons you're a bad influence on society."

A sense of unease plopped itself down on Zane's chest. "Your father wrote a book on moral virtues?"

"Have you ever heard of *The Angel On Your Shoulder?*"

Oh, hell. Her name was Naomi *Tyler.* It was such a common name, he hadn't made the connection.

Zane's mouth went dry, and he croaked, "Your father is Atchison Tyler?"

She rolled over to face him and propped her head on her hand. "The one and only. Do you want to stop sleeping with me now?"

Zane forced a laugh. "Of course not."

Or did he?

"Most guys do when they find out."

"Is that why you didn't tell me you were Senator Tyler's daughter?"

She flashed a guilty smile. "We just met yesterday. I usually make sure a guy likes me before I drop the Atchison Tyler bomb on them."

Zane's head was spinning. She'd dropped a bomb on him, all right, but she had no idea just what a big one it was.

"I can't believe this," he muttered, realizing too late that he'd said it out loud, that it wasn't exactly going to soothe her insecurities about her father.

"I'm sorry. I wanted to have an exciting sex life— at least for a few days."

"How could you not have an exciting sex life? You're beautiful, hot, amazing in bed—"

"Stop. It's really sweet of you to say all that, but I don't have a great track record."

"What do you mean?" he asked, happy to have a distraction from the whole Atchison Tyler news, which was threatening to make him lose his dinner.

"Of those few guys who made it past the news that

they were dating the daughter of America's unofficial authority on morality, none of them were ever able to, um, get me to a certain point of arousal, if you know what I mean."

Zane blinked. "You mean they couldn't make you come?"

She cast her gaze down at the sheets. "You're the first guy who's given me an orgasm."

Zane blinked at the second bomb, careful to hide the fact that he was reeling.

She was twenty-nine years old, and she'd only yesterday had her first with-a-guy orgasm? Suddenly the weight of Naomi's sexual future weighed on his shoulders, and he felt the way he had the day he'd found out his last lover was a supposedly virginal princess.

"It's not your fault you were dating a bunch of idiots who didn't know how to push the right buttons."

She looked him in the eye, and he saw a vulnerability there he'd never seen before. "Thanks, but maybe I was just lousy in bed."

"Baby, you're an amazing lover."

Naomi laughed. "Stop it—I wasn't fishing for compliments."

"You don't have to fish. Not only are you sexy all over, but your enthusiasm is an incredible turn-on. There's not a chance you were lousy in bed."

He tilted her chin up and forced her to see the seriousness in his eyes.

"Guess I just needed to find the right guy," she said.

The right guy. It was a big job, and Zane tended to avoid jobs that involved such heavy emotional baggage. But Naomi looked so different lying in his bed now, so opposite her usual perfectionist, confident self, he only wanted to hold her close, pleasure her until she forgot any stupid notions of not being good enough in bed.

Then he remembered the looming fact of her family name. She was Atchison Tyler's daughter. He was about to break the story that would reveal America's moral authority as a liar and an adulterer. No way around it—he shouldn't be involved with Naomi.

And yet, if he stopped sleeping with her now, there wouldn't be any excuse to make her believe she was the amazing lover he'd just claimed she was. She'd think he was ending their physical relationship because of her father, or because of her imaginary ineptitude in bed—or both. And she'd never guess the truth.

No, it was worse than that. When he broke the story, she'd hate him. She'd think he'd been sleeping with her to get more information on her father, and no amount of protesting would convince her otherwise.

Zane's head-spinning turned into a pounding pressure in his temples.

How could he tell her the truth about her father? And when?

What would he say?

Hey babe, I'm working on a story now that'll ruin your father's career. No amount of image consulting will be able to save your dear old dad after I get finished with him.

Right.

He couldn't tell her tonight. No way, no how.

Maybe tomorrow, once he'd had a chance to think of the right way to say it, when he was sure of all the facts, but even then, he knew what would happen. She'd shoot the messenger.

Maybe it would be better if she learned the truth along with the rest of America—when the story broke. Or was that the coward's way out?

He couldn't think straight, couldn't quite recover from having two bombs dropped on him, one after another.

"So you're not freaked out?" she asked, a smile playing on her lips.

"About what? How bad your ex-boyfriends must have been in bed? No way—it just makes me look that much more talented." He assumed his best Rhett Butler expression, and she laughed.

"I meant about my father. Doesn't it bother you even a little?"

"No," he lied. "Maybe if I met him—and if he started issuing warnings about not defiling his pure, innocent daughter…"

She rolled onto her back, stretching her arms over

her head in a feline movement. "That's me, pure and untouched as the driven snow."

The sheet had slipped down, revealing her breasts. Her nipples were dark, erect, begging for his attention. He slid his hand up her rib cage and cupped her breast, savoring the feel of her soft, hot flesh.

"I guess that makes me the defiler."

She looked at him out of the corner of her eye. "That's okay. I've needed to be properly defiled for a long, long time. So just put my dad—and that whole orgasm-impairment thing—out of your head. I'm sorry I mentioned any of it."

If only he *could* put it out of his head. But now that he knew the truth about her father, he also knew it would be the thing that would drive Naomi out of his life just as quickly as she'd entered it.

And that should have made him happy. It really should have.

So why didn't it?

11

THE PARK WAS CLUTTERED with people, all enjoying a beautiful Sunday morning outdoors. Naomi had to dodge other joggers, bicyclists, in-line skaters and pedestrians, but she was on enough of a runner's high not to mind.

She was feeling rather virtuous for having jogged two entire miles without stopping at a single café. Swimsuit season, here she came. Svelte, toned, graceful…or not. But maybe at least a few pounds thinner. She could live with that.

With her heart pumping and her muscles protesting the exertion, she slowed her pace to a brisk walk as she neared her stopping point at the oak tree. When she was within a few feet of a nice grassy area under the tree where she intended to collapse, she spotted Talia sitting on a bench beside the trail.

"Hey, you missed my Olympic qualifying run."

Talia sighed. "Long night. Sorry I'm late."

"Another one? Who's the lucky guy?"

"Ken, believe it or not."

Talia was wearing her jogging gear but looked

content to stay put, thank God, because runner's high or not, Naomi was beat.

"I hope you're not thinking I'll do another few laps with you," she said for good measure.

"Actually, I was hoping I could talk you into skipping any sweaty activities and having a latte with me." She nodded at the spot next to her on the bench, where a cardboard drink carrier from their favorite coffee shop sat holding two large cups.

"Now you're talking." Naomi took one of the cups and settled onto the bench for a nice, long stay. "I should be stretching right now."

"But then you'd miss the view," Talia said as she eyed a couple of bare-chested college guys jogging by.

"True. So what exactly is the deal with you and Ken?"

"Oh God, he's trying to court me or something. It's *so* 1950s. He wants me to go on a date with him tonight."

"You know, people still do sometimes date before having sex. It's not an unheard-of thing."

"I say, down with dating. If I have to suffer through a crappy dinner and some boring 'so what do you do for a living' conversation just to get laid, I'm going to start hiring gigolos."

Naomi bit her lip to keep from laughing. If she accidentally encouraged her, Talia might actually do it. "Maybe I could run a gigolo service. That could be my next career, after I'm ruined by Zane Underwood and his disaster makeover."

"It's going that badly?"

Their gazes followed an Antonio Banderas lookalike as he jogged past, his brown skin glistening with sweat.

"It's a fun sort of disaster, but still a disaster. Every time I try to work with him, we end up in bed."

"This guy didn't want to be made over in the first place, right?"

"Right. It's a Mediacom-mandated thing."

"Sounds like he's just trying to distract you from your job."

"Absolutely, he is."

"And it's working?"

Naomi got a sinking feeling. "Yes and no. I mean, I think I've got him under control, but I don't know for sure...."

Was she just being played? And did it matter, when she had her own agenda for sleeping with Zane?

"Because your brain is clouded by sex."

"He's just digging his own grave, if that's the case. He's going to lose his job if he doesn't let me do mine."

Talia shrugged. "He's a guy, after all. Maybe he considers the sex part of his makeover."

"I really should stop sleeping with him. I know I'm not orgasm-impaired now, and I *am* getting a little distracted."

"Sure, if you can give up the great sex, go for it. Be a professional kind of girl and stop screwing your client."

"You're not funny. I'll be finished with him in a couple of days anyway, and this will all be moot.... If it isn't already."

She cast a glance at Talia, who narrowed her eyes. "Why would it be?"

"I told him last night about my father, and about the whole orgasm thing."

"Ooh, two blows at once?"

"I didn't plan it that way. I was just so relaxed, I sort of forgot myself."

"How did he react?"

"Completely cool—suspiciously so. I have a feeling he was bothered more than he let on, but he was really sweet about the sex issue."

Talia shrugged. "Hey, maybe you've finally found a guy who can not only make you come, but who isn't intimidated by your father."

"Doubtful, but we'll see tomorrow. I've set him up with an appointment to get his hair cut, and I'm meeting him there."

"I bet you've grown attached to the guy-induced orgasms. I told you they were more fun."

"My orgasms have always been guy-induced. Now they're just being induced by a real guy, live and in the flesh."

"Speaking of the big O, I should mention that Ken

treated me to several last night," Talia said, not sounding as pleased with herself as she should have been.

"And? What's the problem?"

"He did it on the condition that I'd have to go on a real date with him tonight."

"Maybe you'll find out he's smart and funny and interesting, and then you'll have a great sex partner who you can also talk to."

"Right. And maybe he'll be a master chef and professional housekeeper, too."

"Your problem is you expect people to have only one expertise. You act like everyone is a specialist at something in life, and no one can have multiple relationship skills."

"I've dated enough losers to know it's true. Some guys are good for sex, other guys are good for fixing your car, gay guys are good for shopping, and women are good for listening."

Naomi had heard Talia's theory before, and she wasn't buying it. "What about Zane? He's great in bed, he's intelligent and he's fun to talk to."

"He probably has some hidden flaw that negates his secondary talents. Like he secretly writes confession letters to *Rump Rider* magazine, describing warped versions of all his sexual experiences."

"He does not!"

"He'll call you Naughty Naomi in the letter he writes about you, and he'll claim you spoke in tongues every time you climaxed."

"Don't be ridiculous."

And why, Naomi wondered a second too late, was she so vehemently defending Zane?

Talia gave her a look. "You're smitten, aren't you?"

"No, absolutely not." Was she? "It's just like you said. I'm getting great sex for the first time in my life."

And if she was smitten, why didn't she want to admit it to her best friend? Or to herself, for that matter?

"Or is it that you know falling for a guy like Zane would be dangerous?"

"What do you mean?" Naomi asked, though she was afraid she already knew.

"Let's see... He's gorgeous, he's a world-renowned playboy, he's got this fabulous, interesting career, women plot to get his attention wherever he goes.... Is that dangerous enough?"

"That's the beauty of sleeping with him. He's clearly not serious dating material."

"Except that you don't approach guys in such a clinical way. You can't help but let your heart get involved."

Oh hell. Talia was right.

She had let her heart get involved. It had only been two measly days, and already she'd let her silly, traditional, marriage-and-children heart start hoping for something more.

"You're the one who said I should make a booty call!"

"I said *one night*. You sleep with a guy for one

night—you're in, you're out, you're done. *That's* a booty call. You stick around longer and you risk messy emotions spoiling all your fun."

"So what if you're right? What if I am a little smitten?"

Talia gave her a sympathetic look. "Don't feel bad, sweetie. Zane Underwood is a world-class hottie. It could have happened to me, even."

"That doesn't really help."

"Okay, what you do is, you finish your work as his image consultant as quickly as you can, and then you make a clean break."

"Why wait until we're finished working together?" Naomi asked, though the idea of making a clean break made her stomach bunch up in a knot.

"You can't stop sleeping with him now if it's going to create bad blood and make it too hard to finish your work with him."

"Oh, right."

"And no second-guessing! You can't go around wondering what might have been, after the fact. Because common sense should tell you now that the only eventual outcome is a nasty breakup."

Why, for heaven's sake, was Naomi listening to Talia for relationship advice, anyway? It was like going to a Third World dictator for advice on how to run a democracy.

But as soon as the question formed in her head, she knew the answer. She was navigating uncharted territory here. Having sex without commitment, having sex with an inappropriate guy, breaking up to avoid emotional entanglements—this was Talia's territory, and it was only natural to look to her for guidance out of it. Especially since following her advice had gotten Naomi into this uncharted land in the first place.

Well, except following Talia's advice in any romantic matter generally was a bad idea.

And here she was, the queen of self-doubt again, so unsure what to do, she was looking to Talia for decision-making help. She needed help, all right. From a licensed professional.

"You're sitting there second-guessing yourself, aren't you?"

"No. Well, maybe. But thanks for the advice. I need to give this whole thing some more thought. What about your little Ken problem? What are you going to do with him?"

On the field across from them, a game of Ultimate Frisbee had started up. And now bare-chested guys were darting all over the field for the women's viewing pleasure. Naomi couldn't remember the last time she'd seen so many hot-looking guys at the park in one day. Maybe they needed to do Sunday-morning jogging more often.

Talia finally spoke up. "The thing is, I don't care if he's interesting, or a great cook, or anything else. I don't want to get involved."

"Then sounds like you're in the same boat as me. I hope you can row better than I can."

"Actually, I was hoping you could do me a huge favor."

"If it involves sleeping with Ken, forget about it."

"Nothing so complex. I just want you and your sex boy to show up tonight where I'm having dinner with Ken. You two can bump into us and act like you didn't know we were going to be there, and I'll invite you to join us for dinner."

"Why?"

"So I won't have to make small talk with him."

"You are diabolical."

Talia shrugged. "It's one of my finer qualities."

"I'll have to check and see if Zane is available for dinner. We hadn't planned to see each other until tomorrow."

"Oh, right, for some wild after-haircut sex."

"Something like that." Naomi smiled and tossed her empty coffee cup into the recycling can next to their bench.

"You make dirty promises to him if it will get him out to dinner with us tonight."

Naomi doubted any dirty promises would be necessary. She knew how to get her way with Zane, that was for sure. And she was dying to meet this Ken guy, not so much because he'd been her potential booty call, but because he must be some amazing guy to have Talia shaking in her heels.

"I'll see what I can do." Not that it was any huge favor, having to spend another evening with Zane.

But when she imagined the possibilities—and the fact that he might have already skipped the state since learning about her father—she got a queasy feeling that even watching the hottie-filled Ultimate Frisbee game couldn't cure.

TALIA GLANCED AT HER WATCH as discreetly as possible. It was seven o'clock, time for Naomi and her sex boy to arrive. But they were nowhere in sight. Ken was sitting across from her examining his menu, probably ready to launch into intimate conversation as soon as he'd decided between the prime rib and the shrimp scampi. Men were so predictable, she had him pegged as a prime-rib guy.

She looked around the restaurant, a candlelit place of the sort frequented by lovers and anniversary celebrators, and cursed silently at Naomi for not being on time.

"Is something wrong?" Ken asked. "You keep looking around like you're afraid someone might see us."

"Don't be silly—I was just looking for the waitress. I'm dying for a drink." Of hard liquor.

Ken set his menu aside and gave her the look— the "let's get to know each other better" look. It was definitely too late to slip away to the restroom for a nice, long, makeup-freshening session without seem-

ing as though she were trying to avoid him, so Talia
smiled and decided to be proactive.

"So," she said. "Tell me more about yourself—
your family, where you're from, your job, everything."

This strategy had the distinct advantage of keeping her from having to talk, and what guy didn't love
talking about himself?

His expression turned serious. "We can get to all
that later. First, I want to tell you the real reason
we're here tonight."

Oh God, this whole thing had been an act, an
elaborate plot to get her to join some multilevel
marketing scheme.

"I have to tell you, I'm really not interested in sell-
ing anything."

"What?" He blinked, clearly confused.

"Never mind."

"Ever since we slept together six months ago, I've
been thinking about you. And seeing you again,
being with you the past few nights, confirms something important for me."

Their waitress, who clearly had perfect timing, arrived to take their drink orders, then lingered at the
table to give them a detailed overview of the nightly
specials. Talia asked questions about the tilapia and
the chocolate trifle in her last-ditch effort to hold
things up until Naomi arrived, but no such luck.

The waitress left after answering her questions,

and Talia flashed Ken a weak smile. "What were you saying?"

"That I think I'm falling in love with you."

Oh dear God.

See, now these were the disastrous sorts of events that could occur when people were late. If Naomi were here right now, Talia wouldn't be trying to keep a deer-caught-in-headlights expression off her face.

"Have you experienced any head injuries recently?" she blurted.

Ken laughed. "No. Why would you think that?"

"Because you're talking like a crazy person?"

"Is it so hard to believe a guy could fall in love with you?"

Talia opened her mouth to make some snarky comment, but nothing would come out. Instead, Ken's question echoed in her head. *Was* it hard for her to believe a guy could fall in love with her?

"You barely know me. We've slept together— what? Three, four times? I can't even remember."

"Four. Three times last year, and then last night."

"I find it hard to believe you can love anyone you know nothing about."

His gaze penetrated her, and Talia shifted in her seat, suddenly feeling as if he could see things she couldn't.

"I know lots about you."

"Like what?"

"I know you work hard at your job and play hard

in your free time. I know you love pink roses, black-and-white photography, suspense novels and expensive towels. I know you're a coffee connoisseur, and that you care enough about how you look to make most of your indulgences sexual rather than food-oriented."

Talia listened to his list, both amazed and exposed. She couldn't think what to say.

But he continued. "I know you're a passionate woman, and that you have impossibly high standards for yourself and probably everyone around you, which is why you think you could never find one guy that could meet all your needs."

No one—especially no man—had ever paid such close attention to her in such a short length of time. And she felt wildly, impossibly flattered.

An uncontrollable smile curved her lips. "You've been paying attention."

"I'm a quick study of the things and people I find fascinating."

For the first time in a long while, Talia found herself looking across the table at a guy and imagining the possibilities.

Imagining…what if?

"I'm flattered," she said, and she meant it.

And she really, really wished she'd been paying attention, too, that she knew something about Ken besides the myriad amazing ways he knew to pleasure her body.

"Oh my goodness," Talia heard a familiar female voice exclaim.

She looked up to see Naomi doing her best surprised expression. A gorgeous ruffian stood next to her—none other than the infamous Zane Underwood.

"Naomi! What a surprise!"

"I had no idea you'd be here tonight," Naomi said, sounding a bit too rehearsed.

This was where Talia was supposed to invite them to join her and Ken for dinner. But she just couldn't do it now. Instead, she introduced Ken, and Naomi introduced Zane.

And then there were an awkward few seconds where they stared at each other, unsure what to say next. Naomi finally said, "So can we join you?"

"Um, if you don't mind, we're sort of having an intimate dinner alone tonight," Talia surprised herself by saying. "Maybe we can all get together another night."

Zane gave her a strange look, and Naomi smiled a little too widely. "Could I see you in the restroom, please?" Naomi said.

Talia flashed Ken an apologetic smile and stood up. "I'll be right back," she said, then followed Naomi to the restroom.

Once they were alone in front of the mirrors, Talia knew she should have launched right into an explanation of her sudden change of heart, but what could she say? That she wanted to have dinner alone with Ken because he'd taken the time to notice her beloved photography collection? That no guy had ever bothered to look at what hung on her walls before?

"What's going on?" Naomi asked. "I had to drag Zane out to this side of town, and now you don't want us here?"

"Sorry. I guess I wasn't giving Ken a chance, but we talked a little before you got here—late, I might add—and I changed my mind about him."

Naomi's face registered utter and complete shock. "You mean, *you're* smitten now?"

"Smitten is too strong a word for what I am. I'd say that I'm just…open to possibilities."

"Wow."

"I know. It's probably a mistake, but it's not like I haven't made any of those before."

"I'll just ask for a table on the other side of the restaurant. Is that private enough for you?"

"Thanks. I owe you for this."

"So…what do you think of Zane? He's hot, huh?"

"Even hotter in person than on camera! Be careful with him," Talia was compelled to add. She tried not to sound like anyone's mother, but something about the vibe between Zane and Naomi felt combustible.

Naomi gave her an odd look. "Okay Mom, don't worry. I'll be home before midnight, too."

"You know what I mean—guys that hot can leave burns."

"Believe me, I know."

Talia resisted the urge to nag any further. They went back out into the dining area, where the men were engaged in an animated conversation that suspiciously fell silent as they neared the table. When Naomi and Zane had said their goodbyes and set off in search of the hostess, Talia decided she'd better come clean.

"Sorry about that. I sort of arranged for them to show up and rescue me."

"Rescue you from me?"

"It was a bitchy thing to do. I'm sorry."

He smiled. "I forgive you."

"Now tell me something about you."

"What's to tell?"

"Do we have anything in common?"

"My other hobby besides music is photography," he said.

"Oh. Black-and-white?"

"Used to be, but I shoot all digital now, so I convert some to black-and-white, and some I leave in color."

"What do you like to photograph?"

"I do a lot of landscapes, cityscapes, a few portraits."

"What kind of portraits?"

"My family members, their kids."

Ken had a family? The whole idea seemed ludicrous, though Talia couldn't quite say why. Had she just assumed he'd been raised by workers on a stud farm?

"I'd love to photograph you some time," he said.

"You mean like naughty photos? That could be fun." Her insides warmed at the thought.

"How about tomorrow night at my place. I can set up an impromptu studio in my extra room."

Talia could think of worse things to do after work than get naked with Ken. "Sounds good."

"Your friend keeps staring at us through the ficus tree over there," Ken said, nodding in Naomi's direction. "Maybe we should ask them to join us now?"

Talia looked over at Naomi, who quickly looked away. She laughed. "In a few minutes. First, tell me what you and Zane were talking about."

"Wouldn't you like to know."

"I can guess. You were making bets on who's going to get laid first tonight?"

"Is sex all you think about?"

"No, I occasionally think about world peace, too."

"I'm sure you have some interesting ideas on how to achieve it."

"Actually, I think it's impossible, but since you know me so well, you should already know I'm a terribly jaded person."

"I bet I could spend a lifetime getting to know you, and still not know everything."

Talia's hand froze on its way to pick up her drink. She had to will it into motion again, as her thoughts tumbled around the idea that Ken was like no other guy she'd ever met.

"Are you for real?" she blurted.

"I could tell you I am, and you'd probably accuse me of lying. Maybe you should just stick around long enough to find out for yourself how real I am."

Maybe… "You still haven't answered my question. What were you and Zane talking about?"

"I'm a big fan of his. I was just asking him some questions about his work, and he was answering."

"Oh. So you keep up with world events?"

"Yes," he said, grinning. "Like you, I occasionally think about something besides sex."

"If that doesn't make us compatible, then I don't know what does," she said dryly.

"Can you be serious for a few minutes?"

"Depends on how serious you mean. I can't bare my soul, if that's what you're hoping."

"Souls aren't really things to be bared, are they?" he said, more a statement than a question.

"What do you mean?"

"I mean, they're the kind of thing we need to keep wrapped up, protected, only revealed to people we know we can trust."

And that was when Talia got her first glimpse of what must have been Ken's soul. It wasn't at all what she'd expected. Well, actually, she hadn't been *expecting* anything. But now she saw him a little bet-

ter, and she knew that within him lay something a little bit different, a little bit poetic.

"Why is that?"

"Because it's easy to get hurt when we reveal too
much to the wrong people. I'll bet that's happened
to you."

Good bet. Talia had fallen in love exactly once in
her life, and she couldn't have chosen a more wrong
person to bare her soul to.

She shrugged and smiled. "It's happened to everyone, right?"

And true to his poetic self, he didn't push.
"Right."

Talia sipped her drink, comfortable in the quiet
that settled on them. Finding someone like Ken had
not been on her agenda, yet here he was. And even
a girl as world-weary as Talia knew that when you
stumbled upon a diamond in the giant pile of coals,
you didn't toss it aside and continue your search for
adequate coal.

12

ZANE PULLED into the parking lot of Naomi's apartment complex and killed the engine of his BMW. All day, he'd agonized over what to do about _____ nd the Atchison Tyler story. While the firs _____ answer was simple enough on the su _____ sleeping with her—the second half was _____

Should he ruin their perfect evening and tell her what he knew? Prepare her before the story broke? Or would he just be creating more trouble that way?

And following through on the stop-sleeping-with-her part was going to be hell. Not only because he didn't want to stop, but also because she'd take it personally. He hadn't bargained on her calling him today for a personal date, and she'd been so insistent, he hadn't been able to say no. And to make matters worse, he'd loved having dinner with her, meeting her friend Talia, getting a glimpse of Naomi's life from a new angle.

So here they were.

"You want to come up?" she asked.

There was the answer he should have given, and

then there was the answer his guy parts were singing in chorus. "Um," he said, waffling.

"Oh, I keep forgetting to tell you, I snagged you a two o'clock appointment tomorrow at a great salon. I'll call you in the morning with the address, okay?"

"Great." Just freaking great.

"I've got fresh biscotti upstairs, if you want to have some coffee," she said.

Zane smiled. "You don't have to bribe me with sweets to get me into your apartment, you know."

She cocked an eyebrow. "Apparently, I do."

"I'm sorry, I just have a lot of work to do. I'm afraid I'll keep getting further behind if I stay out late again tonight."

"What's all this mysterious 'work' you're doing? Following a hot lead?"

"Something like that," he said as his gut clenched.

"I thought Jack Hiller told me you weren't allowed to work until your makeover is complete."

"He's not assigning me any stories, but that doesn't mean I can't find my own."

"So what are you working on?"

This was where he should tell her the truth. And, he realized then, she deserved to be forewarned.

"It's a political story, actually."

"Oh, then spare me the details. I've had enough politics to last me a lifetime."

"But I think we do need to talk about this." He turned to her, bracing himself for the inevitable.

She flashed a wry grin. "Are you trying to avoid having sex with me now because of what I told you last night?"

"Absolutely not."

"You *are,* aren't you? That's what this is about. I knew it—"

"Naomi, that's not it at all. It's just that your father—"

"My father has nothing to do with my sex life, and if you disregard me just because of him, I'm going to be extremely pissed off."

"No, that's not what I meant." This was going downhill fast.

"Do you have any idea how hard it is to be Atchison Tyler's daughter?"

Zane shook his head. "I can guess."

"It sucks! But finally—finally!—I find a guy who can give me an orgasm, and you're ready to run from my bed before I even get used to having a great sex life."

Oh hell. Zane leaned over and kissed her, if for no other reason than to shut her up. Well, there were other reasons—he was kissing her because he wanted to, because he couldn't stand listening to her sound so miserable, because he wanted her to know exactly how badly he still wanted her.

Naomi clearly was not offended. She slid her hands over his shoulders and pulled him closer, deepened the kiss, tempting him with her tongue until he knew there was no damn way he'd turn down going inside her apartment for biscotti and more.

When they finally came up for air, she was nearly in his lap. Her gaze traveled from his mouth to his eyes, and she gave him a coy look.

"Do you have any idea how adept a girl can get at pleasuring herself when the guys in her life can't do the job?"

Zane's budding erection went full-on. "Why don't you tell me?"

She smiled a slow, sultry smile. "Do you want to watch me touch myself?"

"I wouldn't want you having to do all the work, but it might be nice to see a little skill demonstration."

"Then you'll have to come inside."

"What are we waiting for?"

Zane knew he'd regret it in the morning, but tonight, he had no time for regrets. They got out of the car, and he followed Naomi up the sidewalk to her door. She let them in, and inside, she switched on a light and led him to the kitchen that opened up on the living room. The two rooms were divided by a breakfast bar, which was furnished by two bar stools.

"Have a seat," Naomi said, gesturing to one as she went to the counter. She held up a large plastic Ziploc bag. "Biscotti?"

He smiled. "I guess I should tell you, I'm not

much of a biscotti fan. I just came up here for the sex."

She tossed the bag aside and smiled as she perched herself on the countertop in front of him. "I was hoping you'd say that."

"So, about that skill demonstration you mentioned…"

"I don't usually do it for an audience," she said in a half whisper as she leaned in close to him.

"You never once had an orgasm with a guy before Friday night?"

Naomi shook her head. "You make it sound criminal."

"It should be, for the guys involved. You've really had to take care of yourself for all these years?"

Not that it was any of his business, but the pushy journalist in him couldn't resist asking.

"I guess I'm a freak of nature," she said, spreading her legs until her skirt slid up her thighs.

"You're definitely not a freak of nature."

Naomi laughed. "Too bad there's not an Olympic Games for that kind of thing. I'd finally have a sport I could be competitive in."

"Maybe you could teach me a few things."

"I hate to be the one to break the news, but we've got different equipment. The techniques don't translate very well."

Zane's cock stirred again in his pants, ready for any techniques she was willing to demonstrate. "I meant, you could probably teach me a few things about *your* body, since you're the best expert on it."

A slow smile spread across Naomi's lips. "I'm sure I couldn't teach you anything you don't already know."

"You're giving me too much credit." He trailed his hand up her side, along the dip in her waist and up her rib cage to the soft fullness of her breasts. He brushed against her gently. "I want to watch you," he said.

She closed her eyes, her face soft and vulnerable, as he teased her nipples. Then she slid her hands up her thighs, pushed her skirt all the way up, and pulled her panties down.

Her legs spread wide open in front of him, she gave Zane a tempting view of her pretty pink folds, and it was all he could do not to take her right then and there.

She dipped her fingers inside herself, first one, then two, then three. Then she slipped them back out and began rubbing her clit oh-so-slowly.

He was so mesmerized by the show, he almost didn't notice that she'd opened her eyes and was watching him, watching her.

"I think it's only fair," she finally said, "that if I teach you all my best techniques, you have to teach me yours."

Zane stood up from the bar stool and pulled her tight against him so that she could feel the fullness of his erection. He kissed her with all his pent-up desire.

"I think you've got yourself a deal," he said.

He might have problems on his hands come morning, but tonight, he had only one thing on his mind.

ZANE RANG NAOMI'S DOORBELL and waited, as his insides protested the fact that he was about to say goodbye to her. He'd already seen her once today at the salon, where she'd overseen the chopping off of three inches of his hair, so now he had a new haircut that didn't look bad at all.

He had to admit, Naomi was very good at her job. Even he could see the logic of her argument about why he needed to lose the rebel-without-a-comb look. He didn't necessarily agree with it, but he did want to keep his job, and if looking like a prepschool grad was the way to do it, then what the hell. He'd save his own style for after-work hours.

Naomi'd had to run off to an appointment with a new client right after his haircut, so she'd asked him if he could stop by her place later for a final discussion about his makeover.

Whatever. He didn't have any makeover issues to discuss, but he did want to see her again, which is why he'd agreed to come by. He should have insisted they meet in a public place to avoid a replay of last night, but what could he say? He knew they had private things to discuss.

He'd spent the morning tracking down sources for the Atchison Tyler story, and it looked as if three were willing to talk to him, which meant he could probably break the story by the end of the week.

And permanently end his chances of anything ever happening with him and Naomi again.

The sound of heels clicking on tile could be heard from inside, and then Naomi opened the door. Her sleek brown hair had been swept up on top of her head in a sexy career-girl style, and her pale blue suit hugged curves he realized then he wasn't ready to let go of. She was talking on the phone to someone, but she smiled and waved him in.

"Hey," he said in a stage whisper as he entered.

To the person on the phone, she said, "I hear what you're saying, but it's not going to happen. I can't see you."

Zane went into the living room and sat down on the burgundy couch cluttered with pillows, unable to resist eavesdropping. He sat back, and the pillows nearly swallowed him up.

"I have to go now," she said. "I have a visitor…. No, I'm not going to forgive and forget…. Goodbye," she said and hung up the phone.

She came into the room and sat down near him. "Sorry about that."

"Didn't sound like a client."

She rolled her eyes. "Not a client, just a pain in the ass."

Zane realized he had no claim on Naomi, but some little part of him felt a stab of jealousy for what had sounded like a conversation with a guy.

She smiled as she surveyed his appearance. "You look great!"

"Don't make too big a deal out of it. I may have to mess up my hair or something."

"Okay, okay. I'll pretend you look like something the cat dragged in."

Zane smiled. "Do you have a cat?"

"Just an imaginary one. She's low maintenance, and she never sheds."

"Oh. That's…bizarre."

"You've got to allow a girl a few eccentricities."

"Aren't you worried about your image being compromised?"

She shrugged. "I'm a multifaceted girl. Are you ready for your big test?"

"This won't involve multiple choice questions, will it? Because I'm lousy at those."

"It's more of an oral exam."

"I feel kind of bad telling you this now, but…"

"Don't tell me you returned all the clothes."

"No, the clothes are fine. It's just that this makeover might have been for nothing. I got a call on my cell phone on the way over here from Spectra News Network. I guess word leaked out about my troubles at Mediacom, and now Spectra wants to hire me."

Naomi blinked. "Wow."

"They made an interesting offer. I'll have my agent present it to Jack and see what Mediacom's willing to counter with."

"This is excellent news. You're going to end up being their darling again."

Zane shrugged. "I don't know if I give a damn one way or the other. I guess I've started doing some soul-searching since this whole 'change your image' ultimatum came down, and I've realized it's time for some kind of a change—I just don't know what."

"Maybe Spectra is the change you're looking for. Aren't they based in New York City? Would you move if you took the job?"

Zane nodded. "Looks like I would have to move."

He'd grown up moving all over the world as a navy brat while his father served in the military, and he'd never felt an attachment to one particular place—certainly not sprawling, humid Atlanta. But for reasons he couldn't explain, the idea of leaving here now had him feeling edgy and off center.

Her forehead creased. "Do you have any family here?"

"No, most of my family lives in Maryland now, so I'd actually be a little closer to them in New York."

"Well, whatever you decide, it's been a pleasure working with you." She grinned. "And I mean that in the most literal sense."

"Am I your all-time favorite client?"

"No contest," she said with a little laugh. "I asked you here because I was going to review your on-camera style, but it sounds like you've already got what the networks are looking for."

"Can I call you for emergency image advice if I ever need it?" he joked.

"Absolutely. But for now, I think my work here is done."

"Thank God."

A smile played on Naomi's lips. "Has working with me been that awful?"

He pinned her with a look that should have said it all. "You know that's not true. I just wasn't crazy about being made over against my will."

"I know what you mean. Whatever you do, you'll be a success. You've got that star quality—people can't look away when you're on camera."

"How about off camera?"

She sighed. "I think you know how I feel about your off-camera presence."

"Yeah," he said, feeling an unwelcome tightness in his throat. "Same here."

"I always give my clients a chance to fill out a report card on me," she said, picking up a piece of paper from the coffee table.

She handed it to him, and a glance revealed it to be a survey.

"I can tell you now, you get tens on everything," he said as he set the paper aside.

"Any constructive feedback?"

"You should know, it's pretty unprofessional to sleep with your clients." He grinned, and she slapped him on the leg.

"I'll remember that!" She laughed, then sobered. "Really though, I'm curious, being a person in the business of images—what's your overall impression of me?"

"Polished perfection. If you were a car, you'd be the gleaming showroom model."

She rolled her eyes. "I love it when guys compare me to vehicles."

"Hey, it's an analogy, that's all. But I'm not finished. You project the image of someone who's in control of herself and things around her. You try not to appear too uptight, and sometimes you succeed. You turn heads wherever you go, partly because you dress so well and partly because you're beautiful and well groomed. But none of that has much to do with who you really are."

Naomi propped her head on her hand as she listened. She was trying to appear casual, unmoved by his observations. "You don't think so?"

He shrugged. "Just going by my journalist's instincts."

"So how do my public image and the real me differ?"

"Don't you know?"

"Maybe, maybe not. I think I'm pretty up-front

about who I am, so I'm interested to hear your opinion."

"You've got a lot going on under that polished surface. When I first met you, I thought you were just another high-maintenance babe."

Her eyebrows shot up, and when she recovered, she flashed a wry grin.

Zane continued, possibly digging his own grave, he realized. "I soon saw my error though. You're not high-maintenance so much as you are exacting. You're a perfectionist, but I like that your high standards apply mainly to yourself—not to everyone around you."

She smiled. "Except the people who pay me."

"You may think you're at your best when you're all polish and expensive suits, but I've seen you at your best, and it's when you've let your guard down—when you're not trying to be perfect."

"I don't try to be perfect," she said. "I just aim for my own personal best."

Zane tried not to smile. She took this stuff seriously, no doubt, and he couldn't help finding it all charming. Naomi was his polar opposite. No damn wonder she was so irresistible to him.

He edged closer to her on the couch, then leaned in close. "I'll tell you a secret. You're at your personal best when you're naked in my bed."

"How about naked on my couch?"

His cock stirred at the sexy shift of conversation.

But he'd come here to end their relationship, not prolong it. He'd be a supreme asshole if he slept with her again, knowing he was about to ruin her father's career, knowing he didn't have the spine to tell her the truth.

"How do we always manage to turn these meetings into something sexual?" he said, his tone teasing, his body anything but.

"I guess that's what happens when you base a relationship on sex and business—the two get confused."

"I haven't been confused," he said. "Have you?"

"Maybe a little. This isn't exactly my standard consultant-client arrangement."

"Yeah, to be honest, I've never slept with my image consultant before."

"Because you've never had one before?"

"Oh, right." Part of him wanted to kiss her, and part of him—his damn nagging conscience—wanted to set things straight, once and for all.

"So, if I'm at my best in bed, does that mean I'm in the wrong career field?"

"I was only telling a half-truth. You're at your best all the time. I've never met a woman more polished, intelligent, beautiful and fun than you."

"Now you're just blowing smoke."

"No, I'm being honest. And while I'm being honest…" His gut clenched. "I have to tell you, I think we shouldn't keep doing what we've been doing."

Her smile vanished, but she said, "I agree. I was just trying to figure out how to say the same thing to you."

Zane breathed a sigh of relief. "If we keep going like we have been—"

"Someone's going to get hurt," she filled in for him.

"Exactly."

She smiled, but it had a brittle quality. "I'm glad we agree on this."

There was an awkward silence. Zane had never had to do a sit-down to end a sexual relationship before, but that's what happened when you mixed business with pleasure.

"This is kind of…weird, huh?" Naomi finally said.

"Yeah, I'm used to ending a fling by just not answering phone calls."

She expelled a nervous laugh. "You're my first fling, and probably my last."

I'm going to miss you, he wanted to say. But what purpose would it serve? And was it really true?

Definitely true, and definitely not a good idea to say it.

"I'm honored," he said. "Hope you have a few good memories."

"More than a few."

"Me, too," he said, making the understatement of the year.

"We'd better say 'bye' now before we have any more of those awkward silences."

Zane stood up from the couch and extended a hand to her. When she was standing in front of him, the temptation to take her in his arms and carry her to the bedroom was almost more than he could handle. She was the biggest threat to his unattached lifestyle that he'd ever faced, and he knew he'd be smart to get out while he still could, while the getting out was still easy.

He leaned in and placed a soft, let's-stay-friends kiss on her cheek, careful not to embrace her or touch her more than he would a friend.

"Bye," he said. "Thank you."

"Bye," she said in a soft voice as Zane turned to leave.

His stomach did a flip, and his chest tightened. For a casual, mutually agreed-upon breakup of an affair that had barely gotten started, this was sure as hell feeling like anything but.

13

TALIA UNDRESSED in front of the mirror in Ken's bed-room, checking herself for signs of too much dessert. She wasn't a natural athlete by any means and didn't hold any special affection for sweaty activities that took place outside of bed, but she did give it the old college try when it came to keeping her body up.

And she was lucky. She'd been blessed with a naturally strong figure, not slender, but very well proportioned.

In the other room, she could hear Ken banging around, setting up for their photo session. He claimed his music room was easily converted to a photography studio, and she'd believe it when she saw it.

Talia had always imagined that someday she'd do some boudoir photos to capture the fact that she'd had a great body. It would be something to comfort her in her old age, when even hours at the gym wouldn't be able to save her from the cruel effects of gravity.

But she'd never dated a photographer before,

never really contemplated the fun possibilities of herself naked with a guy and his camera. Sure, she'd played around with her own digital camera and its self-timer for the sake of sending naughty e-mail attachments, but to think of her body raised to the level of fine art… It was an incredible turn-on.

"You ready?" Ken poked his head inside the room, but when he caught sight of her in front of the mirror naked, his gaze darkened.

"Ready as I'll ever be."

Suddenly, she was having a few doubts. What if she looked like a cow on film? Didn't they say the camera adds ten pounds?

But Ken came into the bedroom, his gaze locked on her. "You look incredible," he said, and her doubts began to melt away.

Then he took her in his arms and lifted her onto the dresser, and she couldn't remember what she'd been having doubts about. He pressed between her legs, spread them wide, dipped his thumb down to rub against her clit, and she was suddenly ready for a hell of a lot more than a photo session.

"Do you do this with all your girlfriends?" she asked, breathless.

"Do what?"

"Take their picture?"

"No, and I usually don't have girlfriends."

That was when she realized her slip. Her assumption. *Girlfriend?* Where had that come from?

But then Ken was working some suction magic on her breasts, getting her so worked up she couldn't imagine taking a break for photos, and she decided to let her own mistake slide. What the hell did it matter, when she felt this incredible? She let her head fall back, thrust her breasts harder against his mouth, and sighed.

He made a warm, wet path up her chest and neck to her ear. "You ready to get started?"

"I hope you mean pleasuring me, not photographing me."

He smiled. "I thought it would be nice to get that look of arousal in your photos. You're even more beautiful when you're turned on."

Hmm, interesting. "You mean, you want to stop and do the photo session right now? Isn't that going to be a little hard on you?" she asked as she brushed her hand against his erection.

"I can suffer for the sake of my art," he said in a self-deprecating tone she loved. "And if my suffering becomes too great, I could join in the photo session."

"Take photos of us together?" The possibilities were getting more interesting by the minute.

"Mmm, hmm. If you don't mind sharing the spotlight."

"But, how?"

"I've got a remote control for the camera."

Aroused didn't even begin to describe the rush of

tingly anticipation that hit Talia. "I wouldn't mind sharing the spotlight at all."

He led her by the hand into his extra bedroom, where a black backdrop hung from a stand, and several complicated sets of lights with umbrellas attached dominated much of the space, along with a camera on a tripod.

Centered in front of the backdrop was a chrome chair. "Just sit on that chair, straddling it."

She sat down, her profile facing the camera, and did her best pose, tossing her long hair over her shoulder. "How's this?"

"Beautiful," Ken said as he composed the shot through the camera's viewfinder. "Tilt your chin down a little. Give me that do-me look again." He began snapping shots, and Talia started to relax some more.

After twenty shots or so, he took the chair away and had her sit on the floor on top of the backdrop. Talia's arousal grew with each shot, and by the time he had her posing with her legs spread wide and her girl parts in full view of the camera, she couldn't wait another second for him to join her.

"Come over here," she said after he snapped a shot of her doing her best centerfold impression.

"I was wondering when you were going to invite me."

He stepped out from behind the camera and undressed in a hurry, donned a condom, and knelt beside her. In his palm, he held a tiny remote control, and once he'd pulled her against him, pressed his erection into her from behind, and wrapped his arms around her body, he snapped a shot, then another.

As they began the moves that came so naturally to them, the only thing out of place was the flash of the studio lights, and soon, even that became part of their lovemaking. It even heightened the excitement to have the camera's eye watching, recording their actions to be viewed again later.

Ken pumped into her, his cock stretching her and probing her most secret depths. Then Talia forgot the camera, forgot everything but their bodies, forgot even to worry that she might be exposing too much of herself, too fast.

Soon they were near the edge, then over it, their bodies bucking against the pleasure of their orgasms that overcame them in quick succession. She wasn't even sure whose came first or whose ended last. She knew only that being here, right now, locked together with Ken, their lovemaking recorded for posterity, was the most right place she'd ever been in her life.

SHOPPING FOR SWIMSUITS was definitely not the right way to cheer oneself after a breakup—if Naomi's departure from Zane could even be called that—but she had mistakenly thought shopping of any kind at Neiman Marcus might be good therapy.

She hadn't expected to feel so damn depressed,

and now that she did, she had no doubt Zane would be her last fling.

"Do we have to have swimsuit season?" Naomi asked as she held up a little pair of bikini bottoms that would cover approximately one eighth of her ass.

"If there were no swimsuit season, we wouldn't get to see hot, glistening guys emerging from pools in swim trunks," Talia said as she sorted through a rack of red bikinis looking for her size.

"And what's with that, anyway? Why do guys get to wear baggy, almost-knee-length shorts, while we have to go outdoors with our girl parts covered in glorified rubber bands?"

"It's a man's world," Talia mumbled. "And I, for one, am going to just relax and enjoy the rubber-band season."

"What's going on with you? You seem almost… dreamy."

And Talia was definitely not a dreamy kind of girl.

"I had the most amazing afternoon yesterday."

"This must be related to Ken." Naomi found another not-too-horrifying swimsuit possibility to drape over her arm.

Why on God's earth had hot pants come back in style? No one over a size zero could look good in them. She thought evil thoughts about a certain teen pop star who'd made the style popular again as she moved on to a rack of one-piece suits.

Talia had remained silent for a bit too long, so Naomi glanced up to see that she was wearing a self-satisfied smirk.

"What?" she demanded.

"He's an amateur photographer, I discovered. We had a little photo session together, and it was…" Talia shook her head as if at a loss for words to describe it.

"Hot?" Naomi offered.

"Incendiary. I'm surprised the camera didn't burst into flames."

"Wow. Aren't you afraid he might do something sleazy like post the photos on the Internet?"

Talia shrugged. "I guess he could, but even if he did, it would still be worth it. Having the camera there—it just made the whole thing so much more intense, you know?"

"No, I don't know, but I can use my imagination."

"You should try it!"

"I'll leave the amateur pornography to you."

She shook her head. "It's not porn. He showed me the photos last night on his computer. He's a really talented artist."

"You're behaving in an awfully trusting manner. For you, I mean."

Talia held up a white Brazilian-cut bikini. "You should try this on," she said.

"Sure, maybe if I start jogging everywhere I go. I might be able to pull that off by, like, December."

"Oh, stop it. You have a gorgeous figure. It's just your puritanical streak that makes you think flaunting what you have is shameful."

"No, I'm just all too aware that I'm not eighteen anymore."

"Try it on, and I'll shut up."

Naomi took the swimsuit to appease her, though she was strongly morally opposed to white swimsuits. "Now stop trying to change the subject," she said as they headed for the dressing rooms. "What's really going on with you and Ken?"

"Don't you want to see my photos?" Talia asked. "Ken printed some for me last night on his printer."

"Um, let me see. Do I want to see photos of my best friend naked and doing God knows what? No!"

"I wouldn't show you the really risqué ones, just the modest shots."

"I'll take your word on Ken's artistic skill."

Naomi shut the dressing-room door before Talia could whip out her nudie portfolio. Outside, she could hear Talia entering the dressing room next to hers, then she could see her pink-sandal-clad feet as she closed her dressing room door. Then there was the sound of shuffling, as Naomi undressed and shimmied into her first suit.

It was a black knit string bikini, slightly more bare than she usually went, but not so bare that she'd need a full body wax to wear it. She peered into the three-way mirror and frowned. Was Talia right? Did she subconsciously think there was something inherently wicked about revealing her body?

It sounded crazy, but she had always associated revealing clothes with being a bad girl, and she'd pretty much tried to be a good girl her whole life.

Whatever. Maybe it was just one more of a hundred ways she was warped, but worrying about it was not going to make her buy this *Charlie's Angels* bikini. She took it off and was about to pry herself into the next one when Talia slipped something under the dressing-room wall.

Naomi was almost afraid to look, but she did. On the floor lay a black-and-white photo of Talia from behind. She was sitting on her knees, her hair cascading down her back, her head turned to the side as she looked down. Her rose tattoo, which Naomi rarely glimpsed, was visible just below where her hair fell, and just above her crack.

"Did you know you have a tattoo on your back?" Naomi joked.

"Shut up. Isn't it a great shot?"

"It is. It's gorgeous." It really was. "And now if you're ever in a horrible accident and all that's left to identify you is your ass, the authorities will have a photo to go by."

Naomi pried herself into the white bikini bottoms Talia had picked out, then wrestled with the top.

"You think you're such a comedian." Below the

wall, Naomi could see Talia stepping into a pair of blue bikini bottoms.

"I guess humor's my knee-jerk reaction to seeing my friends naked."

"Spare me the stand-up act and take a look at these."

Two more photos appeared under the wall. One was of Talia—just a head shot, thank God—wearing the most blatant screw-me look Naomi had ever seen. Her face was half cast in shadow and half beautifully sculpted by light.

The other was of Talia and Ken. Again, mercifully just a shoulders-up shot. He was behind her, on the verge of kissing her neck. Both had their eyes closed, and the picture was erotic in an almost tender way. Like she was catching a glimpse of an emotion not normally caught on film.

Love.

A little lump formed in her throat. Was her best friend actually in love?

It was right there in the photo, Talia's face softer and more vulnerable than Naomi had ever seen it before, Talia's neck exposed so intimately, laid so bare for Ken's mouth. Something about the two of them together, some invisible chemistry that only film could see, created a profound, intimate portrait.

"Why the silence?" Talia asked as she kicked the blue bikini bottoms aside.

"Nice photos," Naomi said. An understatement,

but she couldn't exactly point out to Talia that she was in love before Talia herself was ready to admit it—or even realized it.

"I love that one of me and Ken," she said.

"So, you two are getting serious?"

"I don't know what we're doing, but it feels right, so I'm going to keep on doing it."

"Good for you," Naomi said as she looked at herself in the mirror finally, the white bikini revealing more of her than had ever seen sunlight before. And actually, she didn't look bad in it. For a twenty-nine-year-old, she was doing pretty damn good. If she dared to wear this thing in public though, she'd risk getting arrested for indecency. But in private...

An image formed of herself and Zane frolicking on some remote, deserted tropical beach, making love in the surf, walking and talking and playing in the sand. That was the kind of scenario this bikini would be perfect for. It was the one fantasy in which even she could imagine wearing a white swimsuit.

But her relationship with Zane had come to an end, which eliminated the possibility of frolicking with him on remote tropical beaches.

Maybe with some other guy...

She wanted to see her own face transformed by that emotion so clear on Talia's face in the picture. She wanted to be in love.

She wanted to be in love with Zane.

Not in lust, and not just in bed. She wanted the

real thing. He was everything she wanted, and she'd be a fool if she didn't at least let him know how she felt. If she didn't give them a real chance.

Or not. Maybe she was letting the stress of impending swimsuit season go to her head.

Naomi rolled her eyes at herself as she took off the bikini and put it back on the hanger. She had one more to try on, a slightly more conservative model with a retro flower print. After she'd put it on and examined herself in the mirror, she decided it was good enough. Sexy without showing too much.

"I take it by the silence, things aren't going well over there in the bikini department."

"I've found one. It doesn't make me look like a swimsuit model, but without a miracle, it'll have to do. How about you?"

She slid Talia's pictures back under the wall to her and then dressed.

"This little number with the rhinestones works for me. I'll be going glam this summer, I guess."

"You're the only woman I know who can pull off rhinestone sunglasses, so go for it."

A few minutes later, they were both dressed and standing in line to make their purchases, and Naomi was surprised to find that she didn't want to put back the white bikini.

When Talia spotted it hiding under the flower-print one on Naomi's arm, she smiled. "Ooh, you're getting the Brazilian! You should have shown it to me."

Naomi shrugged. "I was almost too embarrassed to show it to myself. I don't know where I'll ever wear the thing."

"I'm sure you can come up with something. I'm a little shocked you're actually going to buy it though. I suggested it as a joke."

"I figured if I don't wear it now, then when? I'm not going to start looking any better in teeny bikinis when I'm forty than I do now."

Talia waved away her concern. "I fully intend to look better at forty. It's one of my life goals."

Naomi didn't even want to touch the subject of life goals for age forty. She'd already screwed up the ones she'd set for this decade.

As they stood in line, her mind kept wandering back to the subject. She was turning thirty, and she'd just let the hottest guy she'd ever met walk out of her life. Somewhere in that whole experience, there was a lesson to be learned.

But what?

14

NAOMI KICKED OFF HER HEELS and collapsed on the sofa, her entire body aching, her brain whirling with clients and meetings and style advice. For the past two days, she'd worked nonstop, her business booming after word had spread that she'd restyled Zane Underwood into a more civilized wolf in sheep's clothing.

And she'd welcomed the distraction. It kept her from thinking too much about the absence of Zane in her life and in her bed.

She grabbed the remote and turned on the TV, realizing she hadn't watched it all week. Tonight, she wanted to kick back, vegetate and watch cheesy sitcoms or bad nighttime dramas. Anything to avoid thinking.

But her TV was already on the news channel, and before she could switch it, she caught a glimpse of Zane.

Zane, looking for all the world like a Greek god come to life, was on her screen talking about the latest issue in the upcoming elections. She wanted to change the channel, but she couldn't stop watching him. He took her breath away—along with her ability to operate a remote control.

He really had followed her advice. His hair tamed, his outfit tasteful and understated, his five o'clock shadow nowhere in sight and his devil-may-care smirk eliminated, he was a new man.

She missed the old one.

She missed Zane.

She missed him like hell.

She wanted him back. Wanted him as more than a lover. Wanted to know if he could give them a chance.

She sat up and leaned her elbows on her knees, watching him with rapt attention without registering a word he said. She watched his mouth—that had given her immeasurable pleasure—watched his subtle expressions, his movements, his eyes.

He was one of the most important elements missing from her life, and if she didn't let him know how she felt, she'd be the world's biggest fool.

She had to talk to him now. Tonight.

She sprang up from the couch, raced into the bedroom to change into jeans and a tank top, then slid into a pair of thong sandals and grabbed her bag to head out the door.

Fifteen minutes and several traffic violations later, she parked in front of Zane's building. Unfortunately, there were no lights in his windows. She got out and went up the steps, buzzed his apartment, but there was no answer.

Damn it.

Of course she should have called first. He was probably working, or out with another woman, or… Her stomach churned at the possibilities.

On impulse, she buzzed the apartment below his.

"Hello?" a man's voice answered.

"Hi, I'm trying to get into the apartment above yours, but my boyfriend isn't home to buzz me in."

"Try the fire escape around back. He leaves his window open," the man said.

Naomi wasn't sure exactly what her plan was, but she headed across the lawn and around to the back, curious to see if Zane really did leave a window standing open. Sure enough…

She hopped onto the fire-escape ladder and pulled herself up to Zane's landing. She knocked on his back door—no answer—then pushed against the screen to see if it was loose. When it popped right out, she blinked at her luck. And a minute later, she was standing inside his kitchen, looking around, wondering if she'd lost her mind.

Naomi felt like a criminal, and her entire body was tense from the idea that she was doing something wrong, entering a place she should not have been. But it wasn't as if she had any nefarious purpose. She simply wanted to say she was sorry.

Since he wasn't here, she'd have to leave a message in the one place she was sure he'd look.

Taking a deep breath, she crossed the room and

entered the living room, then pulled out his desk chair to sit in. His computer was already on, she could tell by the hum of the CPU, the monitor in low-power mode. Naomi moved the mouse, and the monitor came to life again, the screen glowing white.

There was a document already open, something Zane must have been working on earlier. Not wanting to invade his privacy any more than she already had, she tried not to focus her eyes on the words, but rather just moved the mouse arrow to the New Document symbol. Just as she was about to click on it, she glanced down and spotted the words *Atchison Tyler.*

Zane was working on a story about her father?

Too curious not to read more, she allowed her eyes to focus on the rest of the words. The document looked to be a list of notes, probably story research. And when she read the first sentence, "Atchison Tyler likely accepted bribe for 1985 gun bill vote," her stomach did a cartwheel.

What on earth…?

She continued to read. There was one note after another about her father accepting bribes, and then… Her father being spotted entering hotels with various women.

Naomi's breath caught in her throat, and she had to force herself to breathe. Air in, air out. In, out…

She felt her whole body tense as she worried that she might have to run for the bathroom to lose her dinner at any moment.

It couldn't have been true.

Not her father.

He was the last man in the world who'd commit adultery, and these lies, these horrible, disgusting lies, were just a pitiful attempt on Zane's part to revitalize his stupid career.

She blinked away tears and she read the words on the screen again. She hadn't been imagining things. The awful things were all still there, still on Zane's computer.

How could he?

At first, she didn't hear the sound of the key in the lock and the door opening. But then it registered a moment too late, and she looked up to see Zane standing in the doorway.

"Naomi, what are you doing here? How did you get in?" he said, clearly shocked by her presence.

But then her stricken expression must have registered, and his gaze traveled from her to the computer screen.

"How could you believe these lies?" she said, her voice sounding more hysterical than calm.

And how could she have been such a fool to believe that sleeping with a near-stranger could grow into a meaningful relationship?

How could she have been so stupid to let her guard down with a reporter, of all people? She'd been warned, and she knew, growing up in a political family, the damage that could be done.

"We need to talk about this," he said. "I never meant for you to find out this way."

"No? Were you just going to let me see your report on the evening news? Read the headlines on the cover of the newspaper?"

He grimaced. "I wasn't sure how to tell you the truth about your father."

"The truth? You think this is the truth? Have you ever considered that your sources might be lying, that they might have a political agenda?"

He expelled a ragged sigh. "I've considered every angle, Naomi. It's my job. And I've got solid evidence there, not lies."

"You bastard!"

"Naomi, I'm sorry."

The horrible truth came tumbling down on her, one nasty fact after another.

"You slept with me to get closer to my father, didn't you?" Her eyes were burning now, her heart pumping, words scrambling to burst out as her anger grew.

"Absolutely not. I had no idea—"

"You thought you might dig around and find more evidence against him by getting me to let down my guard."

It was all so obvious now. So clear that she was an utter and complete fool.

Naomi shot up from the desk chair and it toppled over behind her. She headed for the door, but Zane blocked her path.

"Once I found out Senator Tyler was your father, I tried to end things between us. But I was weak, and the attraction between us was too damn strong."

"I bet you've been perfecting *that* story since before we even met. Did you arrange for Jack Hiller to hire me? Was that all part of your sleazy plot?"

"No!"

She brushed past him and hurried out the door before he could stop her. Before all the ridiculous hope she'd pinned on their relationship showed on her face.

How could she have come here thinking she and Zane had a real chance? How could she have let herself forget that he was the wolf, and she was the stupid, unsuspecting sheep?

She knew. Her crazy, wanton alter ego had gotten the best of her. Had overtaken her sensible, good-girl instincts.

"Don't leave like this," he said, looking more tired than ashamed.

"Go to hell," she said, then turned and ran away.

NAOMI HAD NEVER UNDERSTOOD before that words could be like a cancer, creeping through a person silently, insinuating into hidden places where they began to eat away at all that had been there before.

She'd spent a night and a day thinking about the notes she'd read on Zane's computer. She'd gone from not believing a word of it, to hating Zane for even suggesting any of it, to wondering if maybe—possibly—any of it might have even a shred of truth. And once she started to wonder, memories began to descend upon her like little bombs.

Her father having furtive phone calls that ended abruptly when she entered the room as a child. Her father slipping silently into the house at night when he thought everyone was asleep. But she'd been awake, in the kitchen to get a drink of water, or sneaking around to investigate a noise—she'd always been a light sleeper—and she'd seen him.

He'd always had some reasonable excuse. He'd been working late, or he'd had a dinner meeting with colleagues, or he'd been at a campaign fundraiser.

And then there were the more painful memories. Her mother's tight expressions when her father entered the room, the cool, chaste relationship they'd always seemed to have…

Not knowing anything different, Naomi hadn't thought it odd that her parents never kissed in front of her, that they didn't hold hands, that their relationship seemed more like a business partnership than a partnership between friends and lovers.

She went to the kitchen and poured herself another cup of coffee. Her fifth, or sixth, or twelfth of the day—she'd lost track. She hadn't eaten since before entering Zane's apartment, and now the combination of caffeine and lack of food had turned her into a live wire, humming with emotional electricity.

Now that the possibilities had taken root in her
mind, she couldn't stop looking for evidence in her
past. And she couldn't put aside the growing sense
of betrayal.

In one fell swoop, Zane, or her father—who-
ever—had managed to unearth all her old feelings of
loss. Her mother disappearing without explanation,
at a time when Naomi had wanted her around.

She understood now that she'd resented her
mother's missionary work, selfish as that made her,
and she'd simultaneously felt guilty for having such
selfish feelings. But it had all been water under the
bridge until last night.

And now she had a hundred more questions than
answers. Like, which were the lies? What was the
truth? How could her father have been so high-and-
mighty, so full of moral outrage about every little
thing, if he was no better than the average slimy politician? And how could he betray her mother, when
she'd given up having a career of her own to support
his?

To think Naomi had felt bad for her father, that
she'd admired his standing by his wife even in her
bizarre absence. Likely he'd been seeing women on
the down-low for years, too ashamed to tell her about
it.

Likely? Yes, Naomi finally admitted to herself, it
very well could be likely. She couldn't tell the difference between lies and truth anymore, and she

knew she had to confront her father before she went insane.

With shaky hands, Naomi put down her coffee cup on the kitchen counter and hurried into the bedroom to dress and clean herself up. Five minutes later, she looked a little less like the basket case she actually was, and she grabbed her purse and keys and headed out the door. It was early evening, and when her father was in town, he could always be found at home after work, perfecting his swing on the backyard putting green.

As she drove, her caffeine-injected brain danced from one half-formed thought to the next. It was much easier than dwelling on any one of her disturbing questions, much easier than imagining what her father's answers might be. Before she knew it, she was standing on the doorstep of the house she'd grown up in, viewing it with new eyes.

No longer was the stately colonial a reminder of her strict but loving childhood. Now it loomed as a symbol of lies, of deceit, of dark truths lurking behind the seemingly happy exterior of her family.

With still-shaky hands, she rang the doorbell, knowing her father probably wouldn't be inside to answer. To her surprise, the door opened after a few seconds, and his surprised face stared back at her.

He smiled. "Hi sweetie, what the heck are you doing ringing the doorbell? Forget your key?"

She shook her head, not realizing the incongruity

of her behavior until he pointed it out to her. "I don't know."

He stepped aside and opened the door wide for her to enter. "Is something the matter?"

God, where to begin? What wasn't the matter?

Naomi didn't answer. Instead, she went down the hallway to the kitchen, which seemed the most appropriate spot for any family drama to unfold, and also had the advantage of housing more coffee. But her hands were too unsteady to pour a cup now, so she pulled out a bar stool and sat on it, then buried her face in her hands.

"Naomi, you're scaring me here. Could you please tell me what's wrong?"

Her father was standing at the counter opposite her when she looked up at him.

"Remember that journalist I was working with? Zane Underwood?"

He frowned. "Yes."

Naomi nodded, more annoyed than ever that her father didn't approve of Zane. That he likely couldn't set aside the fact that their politics differed long enough to be pleased that someone made her happy.

She expelled a pent-up breath. "Zane uncovered some nasty accusations against you, and he's about to go public with a story that could ruin your career."

"What kind of nasty accusations?"

"That you've accepted bribes, that you've committed adultery, that you have a long track record of lying to everyone."

He scoffed. "That's absolutely ridiculous."

"Don't you think you're brushing this off a little too easily?"

Naomi's sense of unease grew. She'd expected her father to react with the sputtering outrage he always exhibited toward injustices. Not this casual dismissal. Something definitely was not right.

He leaned on the counter and gave her his I'm-the-all-knowing-father look. "I learned a long time ago in my political career to have faith that lies would have a way of being revealed as just that—lies."

This from a politician who'd always made a point of cutting off potential controversies at the pass? Who prided himself on his virtually flawless public image?

"Tell me the truth, Dad. Is any of it true? And before you answer, keep in mind that there are witnesses and sources willing to back up Zane's accusations."

Her father's genial expression disappeared. In its place she could see a man who suddenly looked very tired. He ran a hand through his carefully trimmed silver hair and sighed.

In his silence, she heard the ticking of a clock and her own breathing. Amazing that she could still breathe.

"I want you to know, if I've told any untruths, they were to protect you. I've always wanted to protect you."

Naomi almost didn't want to know, but she had to ask. "Protect me from what?"

"From mistakes I've made. This is the last conversation I want to have with you about the subject."

"Which part of it is true?"

Silence.

And then she knew her worst fears were realized. Her father was a total hypocrite.

"Have you ever wondered why your mother went to Venezuela without me?"

"Because she'd always wanted to do missionary work?"

"Your mother knew about my indiscretions. She felt free to leave because there's not much left of our marriage."

Naomi blinked away tears. "But—"

"I'm not making excuses, honey, but your mother and I were never suited to each other. We married too young, and we stayed married because of you."

"So you fooled around on Mom instead of facing up to your mistakes."

"No, I was weak. I betrayed the vows I made to your mother, and I've prayed for forgiveness."

Naomi swallowed the lump in her throat. She would not have an emotional outburst and give her father the satisfaction of comforting her. "What about the other allegations? Did you accept bribes and lie about it later?"

Her father's expression turned even more grim.

He took a deep breath and exhaled. Just when she thought he wasn't going to answer, he made a sweeping gesture around the kitchen. "This is the house you grew up in. Do you love it?"

"Yes."

"So do I. But I made a series of very bad investments in the early 1980s that nearly caused us to lose this house and the entire lifestyle our family enjoyed."

"And that's your excuse?"

A rare look of shame crossed her father's face. "It is absolutely not a valid excuse for what I did. But I guess I was a much weaker man than I thought I was. A powerful lobby offered me an under-the-table deal at a very opportune time for my financial woes, and I accepted it."

Naomi heard herself gasp. She had no idea what to say.

"I'm ashamed, and I'll spend the rest of my life trying to make up for my mistakes. That's why I wrote my book, and that's why I work hard to live a moral life now."

In a matter of minutes, the man she'd set up on a pedestal, the man she'd considered all her life to be a flawless example of how to live, had been brought down to the level of ordinary human. There was nothing extraordinary about Atchison Tyler.

Naomi stood up from the bar stool. "Thank you for being honest. Finally." Though it would have been a hell of a lot more helpful to her when she'd been a miserable teen, constantly trying, and failing, to live up to her mother and father's perfect example.

"I believe I owe the same to your mother. Before the story breaks to the rest of the world. I'll call her today."

"Whatever."

"You will give me the chance to tell her myself, won't you?"

"Of course," she said without any feeling.

She turned and headed for the door, not wanting to see her father looking so dejected, so...human.

And she understood, for the first time, how large he'd loomed in her life for all these years. He was her perfect father, her role model, her impossible example. Now that he could no longer fill those roles, she had a feeling she might finally be able to relax and stop trying to be perfect.

15

ZANE RUBBED HIS HAND across the conference table as he waited for Jack to arrive. The wood was smooth and cool, and it gave him something to focus on besides all his conflicting emotions.

The door opened, and Jack walked in. "Zane, hi. I'm glad you could make it."

"What's up, Jack?"

"Good news. Gil Beringer's been so thrilled with your turnaround, you can go back to reporting internationally if you want to."

Zane's eyebrows shot up. "It's that easy?"

"Yep."

"Or does this have everything to do with the other network's offer?"

Jack made a face and shrugged. "I wouldn't question it if I were you. We want to keep you here, that's for damn sure. And I can guarantee there'll be more money here for you than you can get elsewhere."

Zane sighed, too tired to care about his career. "I guess you've got a deal, then."

Nothing much seemed to matter since the night

Naomi had appeared in his apartment, then stormed out his door. He'd never quite figured out why she'd broken in, but the results had been disastrous, regardless.

It made him crazy that she wouldn't talk to him, wouldn't return his calls—and what could he have said to make things better, anyway?

Nothing.

"Great. I'll let Gil know you're staying. You have anything you need to discuss with me?"

"Actually, I've been gathering facts on a story all week…." He opened his folder containing the notes on the Atchison Tyler story—everything except the accusations of adultery, which he'd decided not to make public—and presented it all to Jack.

"This is unbelievable," Jack said when Zane finished.

"I'd like to go live with it tomorrow morning in front of Tyler's Atlanta office, if you'll give me the okay."

Jack's mouth hung open. "You're sure on all your sources?"

"It's a sound story."

"Then go with it."

Zane should have felt happy, vindicated—something. He should have felt anything besides numb. But he didn't. It wasn't much of a victory when the truth he was reporting was the same truth that would hurt Naomi.

He'd considered giving the scoop to someone else, but in the end, he couldn't. He was the only person he could trust to be fair about it, and he didn't want the adultery accusations going any further than they already had. Bribery was a matter for public record, but he felt he at least owed the courtesy of keeping her father's private life private to Naomi.

So now his career was back on track. It was damn cold comfort when the most incredible woman he'd ever met now hated him for doing his job.

THE DIN OF LUNCHTIME ACTIVITY in the bar soothed Naomi's nerves, and she was happy to not have anyone to talk to at the moment.

Three days had passed since the story of Atchison Tyler's sordid past hit the news, and Naomi was still reeling. Partly from the truth of it, and partly from the fact that Zane had chosen not to go public with the adultery accusations.

She still had no intention of answering his calls. He could make excuses about not having known who her father was, but how could she believe him?

She couldn't.

Except…

One fact kept nagging at her. Zane had never asked her a single question about her dad. He'd never poked or prodded, had never tried to lead the conversation anywhere near that territory. And why wouldn't he have, if he'd known who she really was?

The question was a loose end she hadn't found a way to tie up yet.

Her father was handling the scandal as well as he could, and since he'd been thinking of retiring soon anyway, Naomi suspected he would do just that.

He probably was handling the news better than she had, come to think of it. She'd been edgy and nervous ever since the story had broken. All the reporters calling, waiting outside her apartment, asking question after question, had not helped.

She'd kept her responses to "No comment," and she'd tried to mimic her father's grace-under-pressure expression, but mostly she just wanted it all to end. Soon enough, it would, she knew. There would be new political scandals to distract the public, and her life eventually would get back to normal.

At least that's what she kept telling herself.

She adjusted her skirt on the bar stool and glanced around the bar to see if Jackson had arrived. No sign of him yet.

He'd continued to call her, leave messages for her, and generally grovel to her until she'd agreed to meet him for a drink during lunch. His familiar voice had been such a welcome contrast to the reporters' calls, she couldn't resist.

If nothing else, she figured she could confirm to herself that she and Jackson were finished.

And if not… If there was still something there,

then she'd know. She might be willing to give him another chance.

After all, if there was anything she'd learned from Zane, it was that great sex did not make a relationship. She'd already invested a year in building something with Jackson, and a small part of her wanted to salvage that investment.

A few minutes later, she spotted him sitting at a window table. He must have missed her at the bar and gotten a table. When their eyes met, he flashed a tentative smile.

This was the newly chastened Jackson, the one who'd kept calling even though she'd never returned his calls, the one who'd figured out Naomi was a girl worth begging for.

She couldn't quite decide how she felt about him now. Should she give him a second chance? Did she want to? Or did she just want to get even?

She swallowed her doubt and headed across the room.

The thing about casual flings, Naomi had learned the hard way, was that she wasn't cut out for them. She just didn't have the constitution to fling, apparently.

Since saying goodbye to Zane, she'd lost all enthusiasm for her plan to get even with Jackson by sleeping with him one last time to remind him what he was missing. But she also didn't like to leave loose ends untied, so when he'd called again yesterday, she'd seen it as an opportunity to tie a nice, tidy bow.

Or maybe she'd just lost her freaking mind.

Jackson stood and flashed a wide grin, then gave her a warm kiss on the cheek.

She didn't recoil in disgust, so that had to be some kind of small progress.

"You look amazing," he said as they sat.

"Thanks. I guess being single suits me," she said on impulse.

His smile disappeared. "I'm glad you finally agreed to talk to me. I feel bad about the way we left things, and I've been worried about you since the news hit about your dad."

"I know. I heard your messages."

"I just want to say in person that I'm sorry. I behaved like an ass, and I absolutely deserved what I got. Will you accept my apology?"

Naomi smiled and relaxed a bit. "Yes."

"I ordered your favorite," he said as a waitress set a white wine on the table in front of Naomi.

"Thanks."

His assumption felt so homey and comfortable, and he *had* known exactly what she'd want to drink. Maybe he did deserve a second chance….

"I just opened up my new office right across the street," he said, referring to his architecture business.

He'd been working with another firm for years and had finally gone solo.

"Wow, congratulations. I'd love to see it."

He smiled. "I was hoping you'd say that. So what's been going on with you?"

"I picked up a few new clients, one of them pretty high-profile," she said, feeling vaguely nauseous to talk about Zane. "And I've been getting lots of calls in the past few days."

Naomi examined her physical reaction to Jackson after not having seen him for a while. She didn't exactly want to climb over the table and attack him, but then again she never had. He looked good, with his blond hair clipped short and his designer work clothes selected with care. The first thing that had attracted her to him was his ability to dress well. He'd had style, and she'd liked that he was one person in her life she didn't have to worry about improving.

"You know, there's some extra space in my building. Maybe you should consider opening an office there so you can have a proper place to meet with clients."

She wrinkled her nose. "I doubt I could afford the overhead."

"Actually, I'm already paying rent on the space— it's just an extra office that came with the property I'm renting, so I could give it to you at a bargain price."

Naomi shrugged, her practical-about-love side warring with her practical-about-money side. "Well… I'll take a look."

If she and Jackson could be strictly friends, then maybe his cheap office space in such a prime business location would be a great opportunity for her. But if they were going to give it another go... Better not to play what-if games right now.

She listened as Jackson launched into the details of a library project for the city he'd just taken on, and she felt as if they'd never been apart. It was as though their breakup hadn't even happened, as though she'd never stumbled on Jackson having his late-night rendezvous with her computer. She wasn't sure if she liked the comfortable rhythm of their relationship, or if she found it stifling.

Fifteen minutes later, they'd finished their drinks, and they left the bar to cross the street to Jackson's new office. He led her up a set of stairs and into the gleaming work space that he'd just finished setting up.

"Wow, it looks great in here. Did you hire someone to decorate?"

He shrugged. "No, I just remembered the tips you gave me to improve my last office space, and I implemented them here."

He closed the distance between them and reached out tentatively for her hand. Naomi let him take it, but she stood her ground when he tried to pull her closer.

"What are you doing?"

"Can we pick up where we left off?" he said. "I've missed you like crazy."

She swallowed a lump in her throat.

Did she want to go back to him? Maybe Jackson really was her Mr. Right, and she'd never know for sure unless she gave him another chance.

Maybe Zane had been the catalyst she needed to really let loose with a man who was ready for a commitment. Maybe now Jackson could pleasure her in a way he couldn't have before.

Or maybe this was the chance she'd imagined, the chance to show him what he was missing with her, and then dump him cold.

She looked down at his large hand holding hers, his thumb caressing her skin, and she felt…nothing.

Revenge wasn't worth humiliating herself for. And Jackson wasn't worth wasting another second of her life with.

Their relationship was never going to work, not after she'd felt the kind of intensity that Zane had shown her.

"No, I'm sorry," she finally said. "There's just no way. The office space, us—none of it will ever work."

"But—"

She twisted her hand out of his grasp and edged toward the door. Feeling freer than she had in a long time, certain in the knowledge that if she had to choose between having no relationship and having the kind of tepid one she'd shared with Jackson, she'd take the first option any day.

"I've got to go," she said:

Jackson stared dumbfounded at her, his face registering confusion. "What's wrong?"

"Us. This was a mistake. I shouldn't have met you for drinks, and I shouldn't have come here."

"Then why did you?"

"I thought maybe I wanted to make this work with you, but I see now I was wrong."

"What is this—some kind of punishment for me? You let me think we could get back together, and then you turn cold and bitchy?"

"We're just not right for each other. I'm sorry," she said as she reached the office door and opened it.

"Don't leave without talking," he said, raking his hand through his hair.

"Don't call me anymore. There's nothing else to say except goodbye."

NAOMI SAT AT HER DESK in her favorite purple satin pj's, eating doughnuts and feeling sorry for herself. She clicked the play button on her monitor and watched the Internet video clip of Zane's old news report for what must have been the twentieth time. His cocky attitude, his wild hair, his old leather jacket—she loved it all. She was sorry she'd ever changed a hair of his appearance.

In the week since her meeting with Jackson, she'd started to realize how special what she and Zane had was, and how much she was throwing away by not giving them the chance she'd set out to give them the night she'd broken into his apartment.

When her phone rang, the sound startled her out her trance, and she clicked Pause on the video. She answered the cordless on her desk, and from thousands of miles away, her mother's voice had the same effect on her it always had—instant calming.

"Hi, Mom. How are you?" she said, relief washing over her. She hadn't realized how badly she needed to talk to someone who knew her heart.

"Doing better than you, apparently. You sound like you just lost your favorite pair of shoes or something."

Even on the other side of the world, her mother could read her.

"Not exactly."

"Boy trouble?"

It was just like her mother to try distracting Naomi from ugly truths. She'd never want to talk to Naomi about her father's affairs, but things needed to be said.

"Mom, we need to talk."

"I know, sweetie. I know." Her tone had changed from caring concern to something else. Resignation, maybe.

"I know why you left now. Why you decided to go away on your mission." And if she'd known years ago, it would have made her mother not seem like such an unreliable element of her life.

"I heard, from your father. I'm sorry you had to find out that way. It should have come from one of us."

"It's not really your fault."

Her mother sighed. "I abandoned you there. That's how you feel about my absence, isn't it?"

Tears welled up in Naomi's eyes, and she felt like a big idiot. By-product of being an only child, she supposed. Her mother could transform her into a little girl with one simple question.

"No," she lied. "Well, maybe… Sort of."

"I'm sorry. I should have made it clear it had nothing to do with you."

"I knew that."

"But you needed to hear it from me. I was just so desperate to get away and find myself…."

"Have you? Found yourself, I mean?"

"I think so."

She could see her mother's crooked smile, the one that managed to be sweet and self-deprecating at the same time.

"I miss you," Naomi said.

"I miss you, too. But you know, I'm not the same woman I used to be."

Naomi had seen little changes on her mother's visits home, changes she'd assumed were a natural part of living in a developing country. "I assumed."

"I'm not the perfect political wife anymore. I'm pretty lousy at dutifully smiling and nodding these days."

"What about you and Dad?" Naomi held her breath, dreading and expecting the answer.

"I don't know, sweetie. We've got some work to do."

"But you're staying together?"

"I don't believe divorce would do us much good."

Naomi didn't understand her parents' marriage, and she didn't envy it, but she breathed a sigh of relief to know it would still be there. Selfish, but true.

"I hope things get better between you," she said.

"I want to hear what's got you sounding so down in the dumps."

"It's a guy. I'm in love with him, and I don't know how to tell him."

"You just say it, my dear. It's really very simple."

"But what if he doesn't love me back?"

"Then he's crazy and not worth your time."

Naomi laughed. Sometimes simple wisdom really was the best. "Thanks, Mom."

"The real reason I called is because I want to tell you myself that I'm coming home for good soon."

"Because of the scandal?"

"Because it's time."

"That's great." And it was. Her mother coming home was the best news she'd heard in a long time, Naomi realized. They might never have been close before, but she wanted to see if they could have a better relationship now.

Her mother promised to send an e-mail soon with more details, and they said their goodbyes. When Naomi hung up the phone, she sat staring at Zane's video image frozen on her computer screen.

Zane. Her big looming problem.

Zane, who didn't know the crazy truth—that she'd fallen in love with him.

He was everything she'd ever wanted and more. He went beyond the guy of her dreams and showed her how limited her imagination had been when it came to men and sex. She hadn't known how good it could be until she'd been with Zane.

And now she didn't want anyone else.

What if he loved her, too?

What if he didn't?

If he didn't, she'd die. Or she'd join a convent, or maybe sign on for an Antarctic expedition.

One thing was clear. She was a mess. She'd canceled all her appointments for the week, and she'd developed an obsession with watching the news, hoping to catch a glimpse of Zane.

She couldn't keep doing this.

She couldn't keep living her life without knowing how he felt. Without knowing if she really was crazy to love him, or if they had a chance at happiness together.

But she'd tried calling Zane's apartment, and there'd been no answer for days.

She had to tell him she forgave him for the story— that she knew he had his reasons for reporting it, and that she respected them. And more importantly, she had to tell him how she felt, before she developed a serious case of doughnut ass.

Naomi flipped through her business-card file until she came to Jack Hiller's card. She picked up the phone and dialed his number. After a couple of rings he answered.

"Hi, it's Naomi Tyler. I'm actually trying to get in touch with Zane. I was hoping you know where he is."

"Naomi, hi. He's in Rome right now and won't be back for at least another week."

Rome. For at least another week.

She couldn't wait another week to see Zane.

"Any chance you have his contact information?" she asked, her crazy heart thudding erratically in her chest as a ridiculous notion formed in her head.

"Actually, I do. Let me find it here for you."

Naomi listened to the sound of papers rustling, her whole body tense now, ready to spring into action. Ready to fly to Rome, if that's what she had to do.

16

Rome, Italy

NAOMI HELD ON to the cracked vinyl door handle as
her cab weaved and raced along the crowded streets
of Rome, swerving to miss pedestrians and mopeds
on every block, only occasionally observing traffic
signs. She tried to relax and take in the sights of the
ancient city for the first time, but the cab ride was
making relaxation impossible.

Instead, she focused on the street signs, trying to
figure out if they were getting close to Zane's hotel,
only to find herself baffled that every street seemed
to change names after a handful of blocks.

Finally the cab came to a halt at the curb in front
of a hotel on a busy street, and the address matched
the one Jack Hiller had given her. She climbed out
and handed the driver the amount of euro displayed
on the LCD in the front of the cab, adding a few extra
bills for good measure, and gave the driver her best
"Grazie."

She turned and looked up at the hotel where Zane

was supposedly staying. Here she was, only moments away from possible humiliation, but she couldn't turn back now.

She glanced around at the Italians passing on the street, most clad in spring fashions so up-to-date she hadn't seen them yet in the U.S., and she took a deep breath—a failed attempt to calm the butterflies in her stomach.

She'd definitely lost her mind. She'd started losing it the first time she met Zane, and she could now say with confidence that she was certifiable.

She stepped into the rotating hotel door and found herself in an Old World-elegant lobby, warmly lit by a huge chandelier. She looked at her information about Zane's location, scrawled on a Post-it note, memorized his room number, and headed for the elevator.

A few minutes later, she was standing in front of Zane's door. She knocked and waited. No answer. She knocked again. Still no answer.

She glanced down at the room number on the paper and up at the number on the door to confirm she was in the right place. She was, but apparently, Zane wasn't.

Damn it.

Her visions of a romantic hotel reunion were fading by the second, quickly being replaced by visions of herself alone in Rome feeling like a complete idiot.

Naomi crumpled the paper in her hand and headed back to the lobby. At the reception desk, she made a feeble attempt at asking, *"Parla inglese?"* And the woman at the reception desk did, quite well.

"How can I help you?" the woman said with a smile.

"I'm looking for one of your guests, Zane Underwood? He's not in his room, and I was wondering if you have any idea where he might be."

"Ah, yes. The handsome American."

She flashed a smile that made Naomi wonder if Zane had already worked his bedroom charms on her. A glance at the woman's gold-band-clad ring finger assured her, though, that she already had a guy of her own.

"Have you seen him tonight?"

"He asked me just a short time ago where I would recommend he have dinner. I told him the trattoria on the corner is very good."

She pointed Naomi in the right direction, and Naomi thanked her, then hurried out the door.

Outside again, she wove her way along the crowded sidewalk. Up ahead, she could see a restaurant on the corner, its outdoor tables filled with customers having drinks and people-watching. She scanned the tables, looking for Zane.

And then she spotted him. Every fiber of her being ached to run toward him, dive into his arms, never let anything come between them again. But she did, after all, have an image to maintain. She wasn't going to humiliate herself when there was a chance he wouldn't even want her back.

Sitting alone and sipping from a coffee cup, his wild hair tamed into a sleek professional cut, he looked different, but no less sexy. She wasn't sure it was even possible to remove Zane's potent sex appeal—and who would want to, anyway?

Her nerves had made her forget all the lines she'd practiced in her head for when she finally came face-to-face with him. Now she had no idea what to say, no clue how to act. Casual? How could she act casual when she'd just flown across the Atlantic to see him?

She made her way through the maze of tables to his and, without saying a word, she pulled out a chair. But before she could sit down, he looked up and saw her.

"Naomi!" Zane stood up from his chair, confusion registering on his face.

"I heard you were here and thought I'd stop by," she said, smiling, praying he'd smile back.

"What are you doing in Rome?"

She couldn't play it cool anymore. If she wanted him to understand the depth of her feelings, he had to know she'd flown here to find him. "I was looking for you," she said, her expression sober.

"You didn't come all the way here to find me… did you?" He smiled as if the notion were ridiculous.

He was right. It was. And she didn't care.

"As your image consultant, I couldn't let you take your first trip abroad since that princess scandal alone. I need to be here to make sure you don't create any more international sex scandals."

He gave her a look that said he didn't buy a word of her story. "Tell me why you're really here."

"It was either come here or sit around waiting until you decided to grace Atlanta with your presence again to tell you that I love you."

If ever there was an expression called smoldering, Zane wore it then.

"I wouldn't be creating an international sex scandal if I kissed you right now, would I?" Instead of waiting for her response, he wrapped her into his arms, and she knew she was finally where she belonged.

"Definitely not," she said, right before he covered her mouth with his.

His kiss, his embrace, warmed her to her very soul, left her without a doubt that her overpriced ticket to Rome had been worth the cost, that the riskiest move she'd made in her life had been a smart one.

When they broke the kiss, she saw that people were staring at them, and she didn't care.

"So. Flying to Rome just to tell someone you love them—is this the kind of thing you'd recommend one of your clients to do?"

"Under the right circumstances. If it had the de- sired impact on their public image."

"Is that what this is? Your own personal PR stunt?"

She smiled. "I don't reveal my professional strat- egies to people who aren't paying me."

He gave her a look.

"Okay, maybe I was concerned about my image with you. So did my strategy work?"

He leaned in and kissed her again, this time long, slow and deep. When he finally came up for air, he smiled. "Definitely. The only other thing you could possibly do to improve your image in my eyes now is to get naked in my hotel room."

Naomi's body went on red alert. "That's at the top of my agenda."

He withdrew his wallet from his back pocket, tossed a few bills on the table, then took her hand and led her out of the outdoor dining area toward the hotel.

Soon they were inside the hotel again, and then in the elevator alone together, where he pinned her against the wall and kissed her all the way to his floor.

Naomi had a million things she wanted to say to Zane, to ask him, but suddenly her mind was blank, and she was driven solely by the need to have him inside her again. She'd nearly forgotten the power- ful force of their physical attraction, but now that she was swept up in it again, she couldn't imagine breaking away from it.

When the elevator doors opened, Zane led her off and down the hallway to his room, where he opened the door and pulled her inside. Alone now, he gave her one more kiss.

"I have to tell you," he said, "I've been giving a lot of thought to all this image stuff."

"Oh?" Her job was the last thing she wanted to talk about right now. In fact, she didn't want to talk at all.

"We've spent lots of time talking about how to improve my image," he said. "But I've got some suggestions to improve yours." His wolfish smile appeared, and she was suddenly interested.

"I'm listening," she said, feeling a little breathless.

"These clothes…" He gestured at her outfit. "They've got to go. If you really want to project the image of being my ideal lover, you need to be naked, or at the very least, scantily clad."

His ideal lover? This was getting more interesting by the second.

"I think I can accommodate you," she said as she began unbuttoning her blouse.

"And your hair. It's nice—if you're about to go on the air to do the morning news. But if you want to project a sex-kitten image, you're going to have to mess it up a little."

She smiled. "Of course. Wouldn't want you mistaking me for a news anchor." Her shirt unbuttoned now, she let it fall open as she fluffed her hair a little, then shook her head.

"Is that better?" she asked when she flipped her hair over her shoulder.

"Yeah, but we may need to roll around in bed some before it really achieves the right look."

Naomi took her shoes and pants off, then stood before him in her black lace panties and bra, the very same ones she'd bought to wear for him. "Is this scantily clad enough for you?"

His gaze traveled over her, warming her up to the boiling point. "No, I was wrong," he said as he closed the distance between them. "You definitely need to be naked to project the image I'm looking for."

Then he slid his hands around her waist and up her back. He found the clasp of her bra, opened it, and she let the bra fall to the floor.

Her body, bared to him, ached for more of his skillful touch.

"How am I doing now?" she asked, enjoying his game, but wanting to hurry up and get it over with so they could move on to the real reason they were here.

"This still isn't quite what I have in mind. You need to lose the parochial-school posture…thrust your hip out and tilt your head a little like the vixen I know you are."

Naomi did as he instructed, feeling with the

change of posture a change in her attitude, as well. She'd gone from Naomi Tyler, image consultant and senator's daughter, to Naomi, horny babe in need of hot sex.

Zane was pretty good at this image-makeover stuff.

"If you don't shut up and take your clothes off," she said, "I may have to take matters into my own hands."

He stripped off his shirt in record time, then kicked off his shoes and started working on his pants. "That's a pretty tempting threat," he said.

And in a matter of seconds, he was naked, except for a hurriedly donned condom—pressed against her, then on top of her on the bed. He spread her legs wide and ravished her mouth with a hungry kiss as he pushed himself deep inside her.

Naomi arched her back and savored the delicious pressure of his body enveloped by hers, the sweet invasion that she'd been aching for since the last time they'd been together. She never wanted to ache so badly again, never wanted to wonder again if she'd have Zane in her life.

As if he'd been reading her mind, he paused, still buried deep within her. "There's something we need to settle," he said as he propped his head on one hand and gave her a smile that was maddeningly calm for the sort of situation they were in.

But he was right.

"Which something?" she said, her voice breathless.

"I can't let you fly all the way to Rome and not tell you what I should have told you before I left."

Her throat constricted, and she only managed a whisper. "What's that?"

"I love you, too, Naomi."

She smiled, then laughed. She hadn't realized how badly she'd needed to hear those words.

"And I love you. Now could we please get on with this?" She squirmed beneath him to make her point.

"I've had a lot of time sitting around alone in hotel rooms to think about things—about us—lately."

He traced his finger along her jaw, a sensual smile playing on his lips.

"So have I," she said.

"I hope you've come to the same conclusion I have. I don't want to lose you again."

"I don't want to lose you, either."

"I think we deserve to give us more than just a chance."

"What do you mean?"

"I mean, you may have thought you were making me over," he said, his brown eyes darkening in a way she'd never seen before. "But that's not what you were doing at all."

She was almost afraid to ask, "What was I doing, then?"

"You were showing me what I was missing. You were showing me the possibilities."

She had a feeling she knew what he was talking about. He'd felt that same overwhelming force that had pulled her across the ocean to find him. It was the satisfying clink of two polar opposites finding each other and coming together.

"I know what you mean," she said, unsure what else to say.

"I don't think you do. I've been all over the world, met all kinds of women, and I've had my whole life to figure out exactly what I want."

He dipped his head down and kissed her.

"I want you," he said. "Forever."

Naomi blinked away tears. Again he'd spoken the words she hadn't known how badly she'd wanted to hear.

"You do?" she finally said, her voice barely a whisper.

"This is going to sound crazy…"

She smiled. "Crazy is good."

"Marry me, Naomi."

Suddenly, the sensual agony he'd put her in for this conversation didn't matter. She'd never expected their conversation to take this turn, but now that it had, it seemed the most natural thing in the world.

"Okay," she heard herself say. "Let's do it."

He began moving inside her again. "You're such an impatient girl."

"No," she said, laughing even as she wanted to sigh with the sheer magic he worked on her body. "I meant let's do it—as in get married."

He was right. The words managed to sound both crazy and perfect even as she heard herself say them.

Crazy and perfect—two words that described not just their decision, but their relationship, too, and even their love. Zane was perfect for her in that absolutely imperfect way she never could have understood before she met him.

Their relationship had shown Naomi that her wild, wanton alter ego could find some balance with her good-girl side—that the two parts of her nature could even coexist in harmony. And she'd never been so happy in her life.

Zane kissed her again, then said, "You want to get married right now?"

"No, right now we have a more urgent task to take care of."

He glanced down at her naked body. "Oh, right," he said. "You flew all the way to Rome to have sex with me, didn't you?"

She laughed. "Yeah, so you'd better make this spectacular."

"With you, my love," Zane said, "it couldn't be anything but."

Epilogue

Six months later...

"WE INVITED YOU out to dinner tonight because we have a little announcement," Talia said.

Naomi glanced over at Zane and tried not to smile. If Talia and Ken thought their engagement was some big secret, they were sadly mistaken. For one thing, the two-carat rock suddenly present on Talia's ring finger was a dead giveaway.

"We're getting married," Ken said, his smile infectious.

Naomi tried to act surprised. "That's wonderful!"

"Congratulations!" she and Zane said simultaneously.

Talia's eyes narrowed. "You already knew, didn't you?"

"Well, sort of," Naomi admitted, eyeing the diamond ring, and Talia laughed.

"I couldn't take it off. It's just too pretty."

"This definitely calls for at a toast," Zane said, lifting his glass. "To happy beginnings."

"And happy endings," Naomi added as everyone clinked their glasses together.

She may not have been surprised by the engagement, but she was thrilled for Talia. Seeing an end to her best friend's never-ending pessimism about men was an event she'd hardly expected to witness, and now that she had, she felt a little overwhelmed by optimism.

She felt like anything could happen.

Zane sat his drink back on the table and slipped his hand across her thigh until he found hers. He twined their fingers together in a habit that had become second nature to both of them. Naomi looked at him and smiled.

Zane's hair had grown back to its wild, untamed style—a little too long and unruly—but it was perfect on him, and Naomi wouldn't have dreamed of suggesting he change it again. He'd also slipped back into the habit of wearing black T-shirts and jeans, along with that ancient leather jacket, and she didn't complain, because she preferred him that way.

Sure, her makeover might have turned him into a polished professional, but that wasn't exactly who Zane was.

Thank heaven Mediacom had quickly realized the same thing. Maybe it had been all the comments from viewers—half of America loved the new look, and the other half wanted the old Zane back.

His makeover had definitely given her business

the boost it had needed, and it had given Zane's career an unexpected boost. After all the uproar, Mediacom executives decided Zane was their hottest commodity after all, and they'd offered him a weekly news talk show of his own.

Underwood Reports had just started airing a month ago, but already it was at the top of the ratings for talk shows. Zane was happy because he got to discuss whatever he wanted with whomever he wanted, and Naomi was happy because the show was filmed in Atlanta, so she had him home with her every night.

"I'm afraid we won't be much help with the wedding preparations," Naomi said, and Talia dismissed her comment with a wave.

Naomi and Zane had surprised everyone—including themselves—by deciding to elope in Italy. They'd gotten married in an unofficial Italian ceremony on the Amalfi Coast, then spent the next three weeks wandering around Italy in a rental car that had no air-conditioning.

Their honeymoon had been far sweatier—and more fun—than anything she ever could have imagined. They'd even found a deserted beach where she could wear her white bikini for Zane's eyes only.

"Don't elope," she said. "You'll just piss everyone off, especially your families."

Naomi's father still hadn't completely accepted that she was married, but he'd get there in time. Her relationship with him had been damaged, but they were slowly working it out. She wasn't in any big hurry.

Having finally figured out how to be her own woman, she was having too much fun doing just that to worry about the stick up her dad's ass.

Her mother had surprised everyone by coming back home just in time for Naomi and Zane's stateside reception—held after they'd made their marriage official at the courthouse—then announcing that she'd retired from missionary work.

Zane might have thought his story would damage Naomi's family, but rather the opposite had happened. It had become the catalyst for positive changes, by opening up the door for her parents to start healing and for Naomi to work on having a closer relationship with her mother.

"I don't care who I piss off. I'd be happy eloping," Talia said.

"We're *not* going to elope," Ken said. "I want everyone to see us get married."

Naomi almost expected something to go flying across the table at Ken's head, but instead, Talia smiled and shook her head.

"We've been having the same argument all week, but I think I'll let him win this one. After all, it might be the last argument he ever wins with me."

"Don't count on it, babe," Ken said, and Naomi saw instantly why they were perfect for each other.

They were equals. There weren't many guys out there equal to Talia, but by some miracle, she'd found one.

Naomi took a sip of her drink to hide her shameless grin. If Talia could find her happily-ever-after, then Naomi believed anyone could.

Absolutely anyone.

* * * * *

Look for the next red-hot read from author Jamie Sobrato coming in November 2005 from Harlequin Blaze

HARLEQUIN® *Blaze*™

Three sisters whose power between
the sheets can make men feel better
than they ever have…literally!

Sexual Healing
Her magic touch makes those sheets sizzle

Join bestselling author Dorie Graham as
she tells the tales of women with ability
to heal through sex in

#196 THE MORNING AFTER
August 2005

#202 SO MANY MEN…
September 2005

#208 FAKING IT
October 2005

Be sure to catch this sensual miniseries
from Dorie Graham!

Look for these books at your favorite retail outlet.

www.eHarlequin.com   HBSH0805

Silhouette®
Desire®

Available this August from
Silhouette Desire and *USA TODAY*
bestselling author

Jennifer Greene

HOT TO THE TOUCH
(Silhouette Desire #1670)

Locked in the darkness of his tortured soul and
body, Fox Lockwood has tried to retreat from
the world. Hired to help, massage therapist
Phoebe Schneider relies on her sense of touch
to bring Fox back. But will they be able to keep
their relationship strictly professional once their
connection turns unbelievably hot?

Available wherever Silhouette Books are sold.

Visit Silhouette Books at www.eHarlequin.com

SDHTTT0705

If you enjoyed what you just read,
then we've got an offer you can't resist!

Take 2 bestselling love stories FREE!

Plus get a FREE surprise gift!

Clip this page and mail it to Harlequin Reader Service®

IN U.S.A.	**IN CANADA**
3010 Walden Ave.	P.O. Box 609
P.O. Box 1867	Fort Erie, Ontario
Buffalo, N.Y. 14240-1867	L2A 5X3

YES! Please send me 2 free Harlequin® Blaze™ novels and my free surprise gift. After receiving them, if I don't wish to receive anymore, I can return the shipping statement marked cancel. If I don't cancel, I will receive 6 brand-new novels each month, before they're available in stores! In the U.S.A., bill me at the bargain price of $3.99 plus 25¢ shipping and handling per book and applicable sales tax, if any*. In Canada, bill me at the bargain price of $4.47 plus 25¢ shipping and handling per book and applicable taxes**. That's the complete price and a savings of at least 10% off the cover prices—what a great deal! I understand that accepting the 2 free books and gift places me under no obligation ever to buy any books. I can always return a shipment and cancel at any time. Even if I never buy another book from Harlequin, the 2 free books and gift are mine to keep forever.

151 HDN D7ZZ
351 HDN D72D

Name _____ (PLEASE PRINT)

Address _____ Apt.#

City _____ State/Prov. _____ Zip/Postal Code

Not valid to current Harlequin® Blaze™ subscribers.

Want to try two free books from another series?
Call 1-800-873-8635 or visit www.morefreebooks.com.

* Terms and prices subject to change without notice. Sales tax applicable in N.Y.
** Canadian residents will be charged applicable provincial taxes and GST.
All orders subject to approval. Offer limited to one per household.
® and ™ are registered trademarks owned and used by the trademark owner and/or its licensee.

BLZ05   ©2005 Harlequin Enterprises Limited.

eHARLEQUIN.com

The Ultimate Destination for Women's Fiction

Your favorite authors are just a click away
at www.eHarlequin.com!

- Take a sneak peek at the covers and
  read summaries of **Upcoming Books**

- Choose from over 600
  author **profiles!**

- Chat with your favorite authors
  on our **message boards.**

- Are you an author in the making?
  Get advice from published authors
  in **The Inside Scoop!**

**Learn about your favorite authors
in a fun, interactive setting—
visit www.eHarlequin.com today!**

INTAUTH04R

Silhouette®

Desire®

brings you a fabulous new read
from popular author
Katherine Garbera

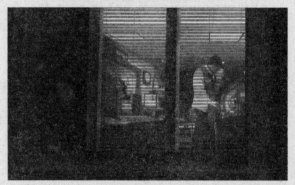

She's an up-and-coming DJ who gives advice
to the lovelorn…but has no time for romance.

He's a hotshot bachelor who's suddenly
intrigued by a voice on the radio.

The late-night airwaves are about to get
a little bit hotter….

ROCK ME ALL NIGHT
August 2005

Available at your favorite retail outlet.

Visit Silhouette Books at www.eHarlequin.com

SDRMAN0705

HARLEQUIN® Blaze™

Women can upgrade their airline seats,
wardrobes and jobs. If only we could
upgrade our men....

The Man-Handlers
Women who know how to get the best from their men

Join author Karen Kendall as she shows us
how three smart women make over their men
until they get newer, sexier versions!

Catch these irresistible men in

#195 WHO'S ON TOP?
August 2005

#201 UNZIPPED?
September 2005

#207 OPEN INVITATION?
October 2005

Don't miss these fun, sexy stories from Karen Kendall!
Look for these books at your favorite retail outlet.

www.eHarlequin.com   HBTMH0805

HARLEQUIN® Blaze™

THRILLS, CHILLS...
AND SEX!

When $4.5 million of their grandfather's stamps
are stolen by a ruthless criminal, sisters Gwen and
Joss Chastain stop at nothing to get them back.

Catch their stories in SEALED WITH A KISS,
a brand-new miniseries from KRISTIN HARDY

#187 CERTIFIED MALE
June 2005

#199 U.S. MALE
August 2005

On sale at your favorite retail outlet.

Be sure to visit www.tryblaze.com
for more great Blaze books!

www.eHarlequin.com   HBUSMALE0805

HARLEQUIN®
Blaze™

COMING NEXT MONTH

#195 WHO'S ON TOP? Karen Kendall
The Man-Handlers, Bk. 1

In this battle between the sexes, they're both determined to win. Jane O'Toole is supposed to be assessing Dominic Sayers's work-related issues, but the sexual offers he delivers make it hard to stay focused. But once they hit the sheets, the real challenge is to see who's the most satisfied…

#196 THE MORNING AFTER Dorie Graham
Sexual Healing, Bk. 1

Not only did he stay until morning, he came back! Nikki McClellan can heal men through sex. And her so-called gift is powerful enough that a single time is all they need. At this rate she's destined to be a one-night wonder…until Dylan Cain. Which is a good thing, because he's so hot, she doesn't want to let him go!

#197 KISS & MAKEUP Alison Kent
Do Not Disturb, Bk. 3

Bartender Shandi Fossey is mixing cool cocktails temporarily at Hush—the hottest hotel in Manhattan. So what's a girl to do when sexy Quentin Marks offers to buy *her* a drink? The famous music producer can open a lot of doors for her—but all she really wants is to enter the door leading to his suite….

#198 TEXAS FIRE Kimberly Raye

Sociology professor Charlene Singer has always believed that it's what's on the outside that counts. That's got her…nowhere. So she's going to change her image and see if she gets any luckier. Only, she soon realizes she'll need more than luck to handle rodeo cowboy Mason McGraw….

#199 U.S. MALE Kristin Hardy
Sealed with a Kiss, Bk. 2

Joss Chastain has a taste for revenge. Her family's stamps worth $4.5 million have been stolen, and Joss will stop at nothing to get them back, even if it means seducing private eye John "Bax" Baxter into helping her. As tensions rise and the chemistry ignites, Joss and Bax must risk everything to outsmart the criminal mastermind…and stay alive.

#200 WHY NOT TONIGHT? Jacquie D'Alessandro
24 Hours: Blackout, Bk. 2

When Adam Clayton fills in at his friend's photography studio, he never dreamed he'd be taking *boudoir photos*—of his old flame! Too bad Mallory *has* a boyfriend—or, at least she *did* before she caught him cheating. She's not heartbroken, but she is angry. Lucky for Adam, a blackout gives him a chance to make her forget anyone but him…

www.eHarlequin.com

HBCNM0705